THE TRAILSMAN

#343

TEXAS HELLIONS

by

Jon Sharpe

A SIGNET

SIGNET
Published by New American Library, a division of
Penguin Group (USA) Inc., 375 Hudson Street,
New York, New York 10014, USA
Penguin Group (Canada), 90 Eglinton Avenue East, Suite 700, Toronto,
Ontario M4P 2Y3, Canada (a division of Pearson Penguin Canada Inc.)
Penguin Books Ltd., 80 Strand, London WC2R 0RL, England
Penguin Ireland, 25 St. Stephen's Green, Dublin 2,
Ireland (a division of Penguin Books Ltd.)
Penguin Group (Australia), 250 Camberwell Road, Camberwell, Victoria 3124,
Australia (a division of Pearson Australia Group Pty. Ltd.)
Penguin Books India Pvt. Ltd., 11 Community Centre, Panchsheel Park,
New Delhi - 110 017, India
Penguin Group (NZ), 67 Apollo Drive, Rosedale, North Shore 0632,
New Zealand (a division of Pearson New Zealand Ltd.)
Penguin Books (South Africa) (Pty.) Ltd., 24 Sturdee Avenue,
Rosebank, Johannesburg 2196, South Africa

Penguin Books Ltd., Registered Offices:
80 Strand, London WC2R 0RL, England

First published by Signet, an imprint of New American Library,
a division of Penguin Group (USA) Inc.

First Printing, May 2010
10 9 8 7 6 5 4 3 2 1

The first chapter of this book previously appeared in *Rocky Mountain Revenge*, the three
hundred forty-second volume in this series.

Copyright © Penguin Group (USA) Inc., 2010
All rights reserved

 REGISTERED TRADEMARK—MARCA REGISTRADA

Printed in the United States of America

The Trailsman

Beginnings . . . they bend the tree and they mark the man. Skye Fargo was born when he was eighteen. Terror was his midwife, vengeance his first cry. Killing spawned Skye Fargo, ruthless, cold-blooded murder. Out of the acrid smoke of gunpowder still hanging in the air, he rose, cried out a promise never forgotten.

The Trailsman they began to call him all across the West: searcher, scout, hunter, the man who could see where others only looked, his skills for hire but not his soul, the man who lived each day to the fullest, yet trailed each tomorrow. Skye Fargo, the Trailsman, the seeker who could take the wildness of a land and the wanting of a woman and make them his own.

*Texas, 1860—Amid the dust and the fury
rides the Trailsman. . . .*

1

Skye Fargo first saw the three men when he came out of the Dallas House. They were coming down the street, two white men and a black, dressed in clothes that would cost most people a year's wages. The black towered over his companions by a good foot and a half and had a body half as wide as a buckboard. They walked past him and went into the hotel and he bent his boots to the nearest saloon, a watering hole with a sign out front that read BULL BY THE HORNS. Grinning, Fargo went in.

The barkeep was heavyset and bald and showed yellow teeth when he smiled.

"What will it be, mister?"

Fargo took out his poke and opened it. The pitiful few coins he had left brought a frown. He would love a bottle and a night of poker and a warm dove on his lap, but that was for those who had money to spare and he sure as hell didn't.

"One drink will have to do."

The bartender poured two fingers' worth and slid the glass across. "If you are looking for work, there's plenty to be had. Dallas is growing like a weed."

"Sure is," Fargo agreed. As frontier towns went, Dallas was downright prosperous. "I saw some men marching in the street earlier," he mentioned.

"That would be the militia. All this talk of secession has everyone worked up. Some think it will be war. What do you think?"

Fargo sipped and sighed as the coffin varnish burned his gullet. "I don't hardly give a damn."

"You haven't picked a side? Down here if you're not for the South you could be tarred and feathered."

"I would like to see someone try." Fargo took another slow slip.

"Bold talk," the barkeep said.

Fargo looked at him. The man blinked, then coughed as if he had something in his throat.

"I didn't mean anything by it. Just making talk, is all."

"I like to drink in peace."

The bartender raised his hands, palms out, and showed his yellow teeth again. "Sure thing." He started to turn, then stopped. "Looks to me like you won't get the chance, though."

Fargo shifted toward the batwings.

The three men he had seen outside the hotel were coming toward him, the two whites in the lead. The wide brims of their hats shadowed their faces and their eyes. The youngest, who wasn't much over twenty and had a thin mustache and no chin to speak of, stopped and said, "You're that scout, aren't you?"

Fargo switched the glass to his left hand and leaned his left elbow on the bar. He lowered his right hand until it brushed his Colt. "Which scout would that be?"

"What do you mean which?"

"There are plenty to go around," Fargo said. "There's Jim Bridger. There's Kit Carson. There's Walker and Colter and others. Which scout did you have in mind?"

The young man glanced at his companion, who also had a thin mustache but could boast a fair chin, and then frowned. "Are you poking fun? You know damn well who I mean. Skye Fargo. The man my pa sent for."

"You would be?"

"Emery Broxton. This here is my brother, Thad. Pa sent us to fetch you to the house."

2

"Your friend there?" Fargo asked, with a nod at the black.

Emery glanced over his shoulder, and snorted. "Friend? Hell, that's just one of our slaves. We call him Chaku. He comes from Africa. He's nothing."

"Looks like something to me," Fargo said.

"Now I know you must be poking fun. Since when do darkies matter? And how did we get on this, anyhow? Come along. We shouldn't keep Pa waiting."

"I'm not done with my drink yet." Fargo only had a sip left, but he could make it two sips if he tried.

"Hell. Finish and we can be on our way."

"They say patience is a virtue."

Emery fidgeted. "You sure as hell are trying mine. All you've done is prick at me, and for no reason."

"I always have a reason," Fargo said. He sipped and had enough left for one more.

Thad chose that moment to say, "We're getting off on the wrong foot, here. My pa sent for you because we need you. We need you bad."

Emery nodded. "Folks say you are the best scout around. Better than Bridger and Carson and . . ." He paused. "Who else was it you said? Walker and some other fellow?"

"If it's the best you want, then you want Bridger," Fargo said. "He's been around longer and knows more than me. Carson would be second best. Walker knows California better and there's a mountain man knows every tree in the central Rockies, but I've been more places than both of them, so we're about tied for third best."

"You're poking fun again, aren't you?"

"Only saying how things are." Fargo savored his last sip. He set the glass down and addressed the black. "What part of Africa?"

Emery made a sound like a goose being strangled. "What the hell are you talking to him for? Didn't you hear me? He's a slave, for God's sake. It's us you have dealings with."

3

"Please, Mr. Fargo," Thad said diplomatically. "Let us take you to our pa. He'll explain everything."

Emery said, "I'm not so sure sending for you was a good notion. I think you just did that to get my goat."

"You're not as dumb as you look," Fargo said.

A red tinge crept from Emery's collar to his brow. He balled his fists and took a step. "I won't be insulted."

"Then you shouldn't open your mouth."

Emery swore and swung.

For Fargo it was like dodging molasses. He sidestepped and drove his left fist into the younger Broxton's gut. Not with all his strength but hard enough that Emery staggered back and lost his balance and would have fallen if Chaku hadn't caught him.

"Here, now! Enough of that," Thad hollered.

Emery wrenched free of Chaku and straightened, snarling, "Let go, damn you. I don't need no darkie helping me." He raised his fists and advanced, but Thad stepped in front of him.

"No."

"Out of the way. You saw what he did. I'll beat him black-and-blue and kick his ribs in."

"Look at him," Thad said.

"What?"

Thad gripped his brother by the shoulder and pointed at Fargo. "Look at him, damn you. *Really* look at him."

Emery did, and some of the red faded.

"You have to able to tell when a man is dangerous and when he's not," Thad said. "This one is as dangerous as they come. You try him and he'll kill you, little brother, and he will do it as slick as you please."

Fargo smiled at Thad. "I reckon you got all the brains."

Thad started to laugh but choked it off and said to Emery, "Listen to me. Forget it. We need him. Whether he is first best

4

or second best or third best is not the issue. He can do it where we can't."

"He made me out to be a fool."

"We can't afford one of your tantrums," Thad said. "Think of Adam and Evie. Think of how much they mean to us."

"She has hair like corn silk."

"Damn it." Thad gripped his brother by the shirt. "Do you want me to tell Pa? Do you honestly want him mad at you?"

"No."

"Then it's over." Thad turned to Fargo. "I'm sorry. He's young and headstrong. And you *did* prod him."

"A little," Fargo conceded.

"If you would be so kind, we'd like to escort you to our home. It's out the south road a ways. We can be there by supper if we leave now."

"I could stand to fill my belly." Fargo let them go out ahead of him. He nodded at Chaku as the big black went to follow the brothers, and Chaku gave him a peculiar look. Fargo caught up and remarked, "You don't say much, do you?"

Chaku didn't say anything.

"Is it that you don't speak the white tongue all that well?"

"I speak it good enough."

Fargo chuckled. "That you do." He offered his hand. "Pleased to make your acquaintance."

Chaku stared at Fargo's hand and then at Fargo. "Why you talk to me? Why you treat me like this?"

"Like what?"

"Like you give any kind of damn. I am no one to you. So why you be so friendly?"

"Mother's milk," Fargo said.

"I had mother. I not friendly as you."

"You have cause not to be. You were taken from your land and dragged over here. I'd like to hear about that sometime."

5

"Why?"

"I was born curious."

"You have big nose, white man. But I do not talk on my past."

"Never?"

"Ever."

Emery and Thad were making for the stable. Emery abruptly stopped and turned and put his hands on his hips. "What the hell is the matter with you? Why are you talking to a slave?"

"There are days when I talk to my horse," Fargo said.

"Damn, you are peculiar. The Negro is nothing. Get that through your noggin. It's us you should be talking to. We're the ones who are hiring you."

"Not yet, you haven't," Fargo reminded him. "And it's your pa who sent for me."

"Quit squabbling," Thad snapped at Emery. "The sooner we get there, the sooner he can be on his way."

Emery muttered and walked on.

"I sure am popular," Fargo said to Chaku, and was rewarded with a hint of a smile.

"He right. You peculiar white man."

"What's so strange about howling at the moon when you're drunk?"

"You drunk now?"

"Sober as a parson." Fargo took a few more strides before saying, "So, what part of Africa are you from?"

"Whites call it Katonzaland. We call something else. It green land. Have much jungle and hills with grass. I miss my land. I miss it very much."

"Is that the name of your tribe? The Katonza?"

"Yes." Chaku smacked a huge fist against his broad chest. "You know what Katonza are?"

"No," Fargo admitted.

"Katonza warriors. We strong tribe. Fight many others. It make us good fighters."

"How in hell did you end up here?" Fargo asked when the big black didn't go on.

A scowl creased Chaku's expressive face. "Arabs."

"Those gents who wear sheets on their heads and ride camels?"

Chaku grunted. "They raid for slaves. Man, woman, child, they take anyone. One night they come my village. They burn huts, shoot warriors who fight, take rest. I try fight and be hit on head. Then I wake I in chains. They march us many days to ocean. Put on ship. Ship bring us to America." His features clouded. "Many die on way. Not enough food. Not enough water."

Fargo could guess the rest. "You were put up for sale and the Broxtons bought you."

"Abe Broxton. The father. He like I big. He bring me to house. He have me learn white talk. He make me wear these." Chaku plucked at his gray jacket. "I not like but must do as—"

"Enough!" Emery had stopped again. "Not another word out of you, do you hear?" he told Chaku. "If the scout has any questions about our family, he can damn well ask us and not a slave."

Fargo said, "Are you anything like your pa?"

"What? No. He likes to say as how he's as different from me as day is from night. Why do you ask?"

"Because if he is, I wouldn't work for him no matter how much he paid me."

That shut Emery up.

At the stable Fargo threw his saddle blanket and saddle on the Ovaro and slipped a bridle on and had to wait while they made the stable man saddle their horses for them. From there they rode to the Dallas House so he could get his saddlebags, bedroll and Henry rifle and pay his bill. It left him a dollar to his name.

The Trinity River flowed through the center of Dallas. They

7

took a road that wound along it until the hustle and bustle were behind them. Little was said. Emery was in a funk. Thad pointed out a few houses along the way and mentioned the settlers who lived in them.

Fargo's interest perked when they passed one where a pretty young woman was hanging clothes on a line. He touched his hat brim and offered his most charming smile, and she blushed.

Two hours later they arrived at a mansion on a low hill overlooking the Trinity.

Fargo no sooner drew rein and dismounted than the front door opened and out came a white-haired man using an uncommonly thick cane. He was old but he was big and he was spry and he came down the steps with the agility of a man half his age and came straight over to the Ovaro.

"Are you Skye Fargo?" he demanded.

Fargo nodded. "Who might you be?" If he had to guess, he would say it must have been Thad and Emery's grandfather.

"I'm the one who is going to bash your brains in," the old man said, and raising his cane, he swung at Fargo's head.

2

To say Fargo was surprised was an understatement. Back-pedaling, he avoided the blow.

The old man came after him, swinging without letup, swinging high and swinging low.

Fargo ducked, dodged, weaved. He glimpsed Emery and Thad, watching and grinning. Why they thought it was so funny, he had no idea. He avoided a thrust at his throat, palmed his Colt and jammed it against his attacker's temple. "Drop the cane, you son of a bitch, or so help me I'll splatter your brains." To his astonishment, the old man did no such thing. Instead, Skye's white-haired attacker chortled.

"Did you see him, boys? Did you see how quick he was?"

"We did, Pa," Thad said.

"He's a regular jackrabbit, Pa," Emery remarked.

Fargo lowered the Colt but held it pointed at the lunatic. "*You're* Abe Broxton? The gent who sent for me?"

"That I am," Abe declared with definite glee. "And you've proven to be everything folks say you are."

Fargo stared at the hardwood cane. "That was a test of some kind?" He didn't know whether to punch the bastard or beat him with his own cudgel.

Abe Broxton nodded. "I had to be sure. Too much is at stake."

"You're making no sense, old man," Fargo said angrily. He had heard some stupid notions in his time, and this was one of them.

"Sure I am," Abe responded, straightening and smoothing his expensive clothes. "It's said that you can take care of yourself. That you're as tough an hombre as was ever born. That you're fast as hell. And that you can shoot the eye out of a squirrel at five hundred yards."

"You shouldn't believe everything you hear."

"I don't. That's why I jumped you. I needed to prove them right or wrong. Had I beaten you, you wouldn't be the man for the job."

"What *is* the job?"

"First things first," Abe said. "Permit me to invite you in for a drink. Once you're comfortable, I'll explain."

Fargo had half a mind to climb on the Ovaro and light a shuck. The old man was half loco. Instead, he slid the Henry from the saddle scabbard and trailed the patriarch up the steps and across the porch and into a wide hall decorated with grand paintings. It was an inkling of what he would find farther in.

"Yes, sir," Broxton was saying. "I'm not one who leaves anything to chance. I make my own luck and I have won the jackpot with you."

"Did you babble when you were in diapers, too?"

Abe Broxton laughed. "You speak your mind. That's good. I've taught my boys to do the same. All three are as outspoken as me."

"Three?" Fargo said.

"The other boy is Adam. He's the reason I sent for you." Abe came to a room and entered, his cane thumping the hardwood floor. He moved to the head of a long mahogany dining table and pulled out a chair and sat. His sons chose chairs on either side of him.

Chaku had disappeared.

Fargo walked to the other end. He leaned the Henry against the table before taking his seat. Making a teepee of his fingers, he waited for the elder Broxton to continue.

Abe was chewing his lower lip. He appeared distracted and gave a start when Thad quietly said, "Pa?"

"What? Oh. Sorry. I was thinking of them. I can't stand it. I can't stand the not knowing."

"Mr. Fargo, Pa," Thad said.

Abe looked down the table. "You must forgive me. At my age my mind wanders sometimes. Not that I can't function. I get around damn good given I can hardly use one of my legs." He gestured at their plush surroundings. "All that you see came from years of hard work. I am a businessman, and damn successful at it. I'm not in the John Jacob Astor class, but we aren't hurting for money."

Fargo had been wondering about something, so he said, "You're a little long in the tooth to have boys so young."

"Emery is twenty-two. Thad is twenty-five. But you're right. I married late in life. I was too busy before that to give any thought to saying I do. Besides, it's not as if I needed a wife. Whores are cheaper and they don't nag you day in and day out."

"You married for love."

Abe's lips pinched together. "And you are a wiseacre, I gather. Why I married is none of your business. It has nothing to do with why you're here."

"Which is?"

"Adam and his wife, Eve. Her real name is Evie but I call her Eve for short. I used to tease him about it. It's like a man named Sam marrying a gal named Delilah."

"A name is a name."

"Yes, yes, of course." Abe drummed his fingers on the table. "I don't quite know what to make of you. Usually I am good at reading people, but you are a mystery. You're not what I expected. You think more than most. Or maybe I only think you think and you're as dumb as a stump."

"This stump would like you to get to the point, you old goat."

Emery glared and went to rise, but Thad grabbed his arm. "Show some respect when you talk to him. He's our pa and we won't abide him being insulted."

"It's all right," Abe said. "Mr. Fargo is justified. He's come a long way. I'd imagine he's tired and hungry. Thad, go tell the cook to whip up a plate and bring it pronto." Abe settled back and folded his hands in his lap. "All right. To the point. Adam and Eve left for Santa Fe over a month ago and disappeared. I'd like you to find them, or to find out what became of them, which amounts to the same thing."

"They went by wagon or they rode?" Fargo asked.

"Conestoga."

"So they signed on with a wagon train," Fargo said. It was what anyone with any lick of sense would do, for mutual protection from hostiles, if nothing else.

"No. They went by themselves."

"Not too smart," Fargo said.

"My sentiments as well. I tried to talk them out of it. I warned them there was safety in numbers. But the next train wasn't due to leave for a couple of weeks and they didn't want to wait that long." Abe splayed his fingers and placed them on the edge of the table. "They figured they could handle most anything."

If Fargo had a dollar for every overconfident jackass who went and got him- or herself killed, he could afford to live in a mansion as fine as the Broxtons'. "At least tell me they planned to stick to the main roads." The logical thing for them to do was head north to the Santa Fe Trail and then head west to Santa Fe.

"Afraid not. They wanted to get there as soon as they could." Abe Broxton paused. "They headed west across the Staked Plain."

Fargo swore. The Staked Plain, as it was called, was a region made up of much of west Texas and a large chunk of New Mexico Territory. It wasn't a plain so much as an escarpment. Thousands of square miles with little water and not much game. Hardly any whites lived there. The Comanches roamed it, though. So did the Kiowas. Outlaws liked to hide out in its recesses. Summed up, the Staked Plain was as dangerous a place as could be, and no place for amateurs. "This Adam of yours is an idiot."

Abe colored. "He doesn't take advice well. He's young and thinks he knows better than everyone." He ran a hand through his shock of white hair. "The young always think they're invincible. You try to warn them. You offer the benefit of your years, but it goes in one ear and out the other."

Thad came back in and took his seat. "The cook says she will hurry it along, Pa. Shouldn't be but a couple of minutes."

"Good."

"Have you contacted the law?" Fargo asked.

"I did," Abe said. "The marshal can't do anything unless a crime is committed within the city limits. The sheriff has jurisdiction as far as the county line and has asked around, and as far as we can tell, Adam and his wife made it out of the county in one piece."

"What about the Rangers?"

"You would think they would show more concern than they did. They said there's no evidence of a crime. I practically begged and they said they would send a man when they got the chance, and then in the very next breath they told me that I might want to look into it myself since it could be a while before a Ranger shows up."

"That was when you sent for me."

Abe nodded. "I figure if anyone can find them, it's someone like you. Someone who knows the wilds. Someone who knows Indians. Someone who can track an ant back to an anthill."

"Only big ants," Fargo said.

Abe learned forward. "Will you do it? Will you help an

13

old man in his hour of need? I love that boy, Fargo. I love all three of my sons. They are the apples of my eye and I'm not ashamed to admit it."

Fargo wrestled with himself. The odds of finding the young couple alive were slim. And he didn't much like the Broxtons. But Abe was right about one thing. If anyone could find them, he was the one.

"You hesitate?" Abe noticed. "It can't be you're scared of Injuns. Word is, you don't know the meaning of fear."

"The word is wrong," Fargo said. "But that's not it. It could be you will waste your money."

"I need to try. I need to know. One way or the other. Do you understand?" Abe clasped his hands in appeal. "*I need to know.*"

"Damn," Fargo said.

"I take it that is a yes?"

"It will cost you. I could be weeks at it. And there's a chance"—a very good chance, Fargo mentally noted—"that I won't make it back out alive."

"Name your price."

"A thousand dollars. Half in advance. The other half whether I find them or not."

Emery half came out of his chair. "A thousand dollars? Hell, I'd do it for that much."

"Shut up, boy," Abe said. "Fargo, here, is one of the best trackers breathing. You couldn't find your ass in the dark unless a lamp was on."

"That's cruel, Pa."

Abe's eyebrows climbed toward his hair. "God, you take after your mother. She about made me want to climb walls saying silly things like that." He turned back to Fargo. "We have a deal, then, sir. I will go get the money out of my safe while you eat."

A young black woman in a uniform come in through a far door and approached bearing a silver tray heaped with food.

14

Fargo's stomach rumbled, reminding him of how long it had been since he ate last.

Bracing himself on his cane, Abe stood. "Emery and Thad, you will come with me." He nodded at the servant. "Rohesia, whatever my guest wants, you see that he gets it, hear?"

"Yes, Mr. Broxton."

The father clomped out, his sons at his heels. Emery stopped in the doorway and glanced back, his dislike as plain as his nose.

Fargo grinned and waved.

Rohesia placed the tray in front of him and stepped back. "You heard Mr. Broxton, sir. Is there anything I can do for you?"

Fargo looked at her. She had lustrous black hair that glistened in the sunlight spilling in the window. Her uniform was loose-fitting but not so loose that it hid the enticing slope of her breasts and the fullness of her thighs. She had high cheekbones and full lips and a nose that turned up at the tip. He grinned and said, "There is something I would like, yes."

"What would it be?"

"You."

Rohesia stiffened. "I'm not that kind of woman, sir."

"You don't like men?"

"Of course I do—" She caught herself. "What I meant to say, sir, is that guest or not, Mr. Broxton or not, I won't do that with you."

"Do what?"

Rohesia opened her mouth but closed it again.

"You're a fine-looking woman and I'd like to spend some time with you, is all," Fargo clarified. "Go for a walk. Talk. Do whatever you want."

"Mr. Broxton wouldn't allow it. He doesn't like for his slaves to mix with the white folks. He calls it unseemly."

Fargo bent toward her and lowered his voice. "I won't tell him if you don't. How about if we go for a stroll after the sun goes down?"

"I can't."

"You have a husband?"

"No."

"Someone you're fond of."

"Not that way, no."

"Then you can if you want. Think it over. I figure to stay overnight." Fargo picked up a fork and a knife. A half-inch-thick slab of steak rimmed with fat made his mouth water. "Thank the cook for the food." He cut into the meat and red juice dripped out.

Rohesia took a few steps and then stopped. She seemed to be debating whether to say something and finally did. "I sort of like you. You're friendly and you're handsome and you don't treat me like most whites do." She gazed almost fearfully about the room as if to ensure that no one could overhear. Then she whispered, "Be careful. It's not what you think."

With that, she walked out.

3

Fargo couldn't sleep. He tried but all he did was toss and fidget and then lay on his back and stare at the ceiling. Finally he had had enough. He sat up, tugged his boots on, donned his hat, strapped his gun belt around his waist and went out.

His room was at the rear of the mansion on the ground floor. The house was quiet. The Broxtons had turned in early and the servants were in their quarters.

He went down the hall to the back door and stepped out into a warm, muggy night.

It felt good to be outside. He never had liked being cooped up. To him, being in a room was like being in a box. He preferred wide-open spaces. Yet another reason he could only take civilization in small doses.

Fargo stretched and gazed at the plentitude of sparkling stars. Texas sky reminded him of the sky in the Flathead Lake country up near Canada. Somehow there seemed to be more of it.

He strolled toward a rose garden. The plants were a riot of thorns and flowers. A path wound among them. He rounded a bend and then another, and drew up.

A short way off stood a dogwood tree. Under it a figure moved, pacing back and forth.

Fargo stood stock-still. Whoever it was hadn't noticed him. He couldn't tell if it was a man or a woman until the figure stepped out from under the dogwood.

Bathed in starlight, Rohesia gazed skyward and let out a sigh.

Fargo imagined that, like him, she couldn't sleep and had come out for some fresh air. Now they could get better acquainted. He adjusted his red bandanna and plastered his most charming smile on his face and was set to go over to her when a silhouette detached itself from the darkness. It moved so swiftly and so silently that he swooped his hand to his Colt, thinking it might be a hostile.

It was Chaku. The giant Katonza wore a loincloth and nothing else.

Rohesia must have sensed him because she turned. Her arms flew wide and she ran to him and they enfolded each other. She raised her lips to his.

"Hell," Fargo said. He reckoned he should quietly back away and leave them be, but no sooner did he start to turn than Chaku whirled and stepped in front of Rohesia as if to protect her.

"You."

"Me," Fargo said.

"Come here."

Fargo didn't like the Katonza's tone, but he hooked his thumbs in his gun belt and ambled over. Rohesia poked her head from behind Chaku and whispered something.

"What you do here?" Chaku demanded. He was balanced on the balls of his feet as if about to spring.

"Out for a stroll. I couldn't sleep."

"You're not spying on us?" Rohesia asked fearfully.

"Why in hell would I do that? What you two do is your business," Fargo replied.

"Maybe you watch us for Broxtons," Chaku said, spreading his tree-trunk arms wide. "Maybe you tell them of us."

Fargo went to say that he wouldn't do any such thing when suddenly the Katonza was on him. He was gripped in a bear hug and lifted bodily off the ground as effortlessly as he might lift a child's paper doll. It happened so fast he had no time to dodge or draw. "Let go, damn it."

"I not let you tell," Chaku growled, and squeezed.

It was like being caught in a vise. Pain shot from Fargo's back clear down to his toes. He struggled to free his arms but couldn't. The pain worsened. He kicked at Chaku's legs, but he might as well be kicking twin trees. The pressure became unbearable. It felt as if his ribs were going to shatter. In desperation Fargo did the only thing he could think of; he whipped his head back and smashed his forehead against the warrior's chin. For most that would be enough. But all Chaku did was grunt and squeeze harder.

Fargo was close to blacking out. He slammed his forehead into the Katonza a second time with no more effect than the first. There was a roaring in his ears, as of rapids frothing through boulders. He drove his knee up and into the loincloth.

Chaku swayed, and went on about the business of crushing the life from Fargo's body.

Hissing in fury as much as pain, Fargo drew his head back again. This time he would break the Katonza's nose. But before he could slam his head forward, an unlikely savior came to his aid.

"No, Chaku," Rohesia said softly, placing her hand on the giant's arm. "This isn't right. Let him go."

Chaku looked down at her.

"Please. For me. He's not our enemy. Even if he was spying on us, he was doing it because he's interested in me. He told me so, earlier."

Fargo couldn't believe his ears. "Are you trying to get me killed?" he puffed, and was relieved when the vise slackened.

"He's not our enemy," Rohesia was saying to her lover. "It's the Broxtons we have to watch out for."

"That you do," said a mocking voice, and toward them

stalked Emery Broxton. He was holding a rifle, which he wedged to his shoulder. "Put the scout down, darkie, or I'll kill you where you stand."

"No!" Rohesia cried, moving between them.

"No," Fargo echoed, but only the Katonza heard him.

Emery sighted down the barrel. "Girl, get out of the way. Pa will take a switch to me if I shoot you by accident. You're one of his favorites."

"There's no need to shoot anyone," Rohesia said. "We'll do whatever you want."

"What I want," Emery snapped, "is for that damned Kabonga or whatever the hell he is to let go of Fargo. I won't ask again. I will count to five and then shoot him between the eyes. Just see if I don't." He paused. "One."

Rohesia turned to Chaku. "Please," she said, and cupped his cheeks with her hands. "Please," she said again.

Fargo's boots touched the ground. There was a rush of blood to his head. He thought he was going to pass out, but after a few moments the stars stopped spinning. "Damn."

"Are you all right?" Emery Broxton asked.

"It was nothing," Fargo lied.

"Didn't look like nothing to me. Besides, he's a slave. Slaves ought to know better than to manhandle a guest. And blacks ought to know better than to mistreat their masters."

"I'm no one's master," Fargo said.

"You're white and that's enough." Emery sidestepped so he had a clear shot at Chaku. "Now, suppose one of you two darkies tell me what in hell you're doing out here at this time of night? You know the rules."

"I was restless and came out for a walk and I ran into Chaku and Mr. Fargo," Rohesia said. "That's all there is to it."

"What do you take me for, girl? I might be young but I'm not stupid. You came out here to meet Fargo and the Kabonga didn't like it."

"What?" both Fargo and Rohesia said at the same time.

"Your heard me," Emery said. "I saw how you looked at her when she brought the food. You like a little dark meat now and then."

"I am a lady," Rohesia said.

"Sure you are," Emery replied. "The only real lady I ever knew was my ma. You wouldn't know the meaning of the word."

Fargo had recovered sufficiently to move past Rohesia and stand in front of the rifle's muzzle. "Unless you want to ruin any chance there is of finding your brother, you better lower that thing and go back inside."

"No one tells me what to do," Emery said. "Not on our own land, they don't. And not when it's about our servants."

Fargo had had enough. He sidestepped and grabbed the barrel and shoved it at the stars even as he drew the Colt. Emery had the good sense to imitate stone. "Listen to me, boy. I appreciate you thinking I needed your help, but you've got it all wrong."

"Let go of my gun."

"Chaku had the wrong idea, is all. That's why he had me in a bear hug. I've already forgotten about it and so should you."

"I will if you say but I can't forget the other thing."

"Other thing?" Fargo repeated.

Emery nodded at Chaku and Rohesia. "Him and her. The maid and the manservant. My pa doesn't like the darkies to socialize, as he calls it. He says it gives them notions they shouldn't have."

"If I ask you not to tell him, will you keep it to yourself?"

"You ask an awful lot for a man who punched me today. But I'll do it on one condition."

"Name it."

"Take me with you in the morning."

Fargo almost said that it would be a cold day in hell before he would hinder himself with a greenhorn, but then

Emery might run to his pa about Chaku and Rohesia. "I always work alone," he hedged. Which wasn't entirely true.

"Make an exception. I don't mind long spells in the saddle and I can shoot fairly straight and I promise to do as you say. You can't ask for more than that."

"I could ask for someone who knows Comanche country. I could ask for someone who has fought Apaches. I could ask for someone who can live off the land and won't die of thirst if we have to go without water for a spell."

"I am tougher than I look."

"You wouldn't stand a prayer against a Comanche or a Kiowa."

"Damn it, Fargo, he's my brother. Adam and me were always close. A lot closer than Thad and me. I haven't been able to sleep much since he disappeared. Which is why I was out here walking tonight."

The last thing Fargo wanted to do was say yes. "I can do without having to bury you."

Emery gripped Fargo's wrist. "Didn't you hear me? Adam is my *brother*. Maybe that doesn't mean much to you, but I would do anything for him and he would do anything for me. I need to see with my own eyes that he's gone for good. Otherwise I won't be able to sleep a lick the rest of my days."

Fargo was sure he was exaggerating. "You would have to clear it with your pa."

"If he says yes, you'll let me?"

Fargo deemed it unlikely enough that he confidently replied, "Sure. We'll need a packhorse and grub so you don't starve."

Emery grinned excitedly. "I'll go talk to Pa right now. He's probably asleep but this is worth waking him."

"You do that." Fargo reckoned that Abe would be angry at being woken up and doubly likely to say no. "I'll be inside in a bit."

Chuckling to himself, Emery spun and hurried off. He had forgotten all about Chaku and Rohesia.

Fargo hadn't. He turned. "You done trying to crush me?"

"You helped us," Chaku said. "Why?"

"I think I know." Rohesia smiled and gently placed her hand on Fargo's arm. "I thank you. I'm sorry for how Chaku acted. He thought he was protecting me."

Fargo pointed at her and at the Katonza. "How long?"

"About a month now. Mr. Broxton would have a fit if he found out, so we sneak around behind his back." She clasped Chaku's huge hand in hers. "I never met a man like him. He brings something out in me I didn't know was there."

"He's one lucky hombre."

"Thank you. I hope you find a woman of your own someday so you can have a house and children and all the rest."

Fargo snorted. "I won't be ready to set down roots until I have one foot in the grave."

"That's silly. Every man wants a home and a family."

Fargo didn't argue the point. Instead he touched his hat brim and nodded at Chaku and made for the mansion. Instead of returning to his room, he found his way to the kitchen. A lamp was lit but no one was there. In the pantry he found a loaf of corn bread and was contemplating helping himself to a few slices when he spied a mince pie. Carrying the pie out, he set it on the counter and rummaged in the drawers until he came across a knife. He cut a large piece, sat at the table and treated himself.

He tried not to think of what was in store. Days and weeks of hard travel across a hard land roamed by hard men who would kill him as soon as look at him. Water holes were few and far between. Game was scarce in parts. Meat for the supper pot would prove a challenge.

Fargo liked the pie. Whoever had baked it had mixed bits of apple and raisins. It was downright delicious.

From somewhere on the second or third floor came a whoop and then the pounding of boots on the stairs. Someone ran the length of the hall and out the back door. A minute later the back door slammed again and the boots pounded toward the kitchen.

The doorway framed Emery Broxton. Beaming happily, he declared, "I can hardly believe it!"

"No," Fargo said.

"Yes!"

"Don't tell me," Fargo said.

"I asked Pa and he says I can go. Isn't that great?"

"Are you sure he was awake?"

Yipping merrily, Emery started to turn but stopped. "Oh. I almost forgot. Pa says Chaku has to go with us."

"Why?"

"To watch out for me, was how Pa put it. Chaku is hugely strong and as tough as anything."

"I noticed."

"Pa says that's how it has to be if you want to be paid the full thousand. We'll be packed and ready when the rooster crows." Emery grinned and hastened away.

"Son of a bitch," Fargo said.

4

The first days were uneventful. Each was much the same. They woke up at first light—or at least Fargo and Chaku did and then Fargo had to practically kick Emery out of his blankets. They rekindled the fire—or Fargo or Chaku did, since Emery couldn't get a fire going if his life depended on it. They rode until noon, stopping for short rests if the horses needed it. Then they pushed on until near sunset and cooked supper—or Fargo or Chaku did, since Emery had never had to so much as heat a pan of water growing up; servants did everything for him.

As if all of this wasn't enough to grate on Fargo's patience, Emery wouldn't shut up. He flapped his gums worse than a town gossip, about anything and everything. He couldn't just thank Fargo once for letting him come along; Emery thanked him five times an hour. It finally got to the point where Fargo drew rein and shifted in the saddle and said, "If you thank me one more time, I'll by God shoot you."

Listening to the kid prattle—and Fargo thought of him as a kid even though Emery was a grown man—Fargo got a good notion of what Emery was like. Emery was spoiled. He was lazy. He was so used to being waited on hand and foot that he thought it was the natural order of things. He was next to useless at just about everything except talking someone's ears off. He could shoot fair enough with the hunting rifle he had brought but only because he liked to spend time, as Emery put it, "blowing the hell out of birds and snakes and such for the fun of it."

"I bet the birds and snakes and such think it's a lot of fun, too," Fargo had responded.

Emery laughed his annoying laugh. "You say the strangest things. Birds and snakes don't think. They don't hardly have brains."

"There's a lot of that going around."

Emery laughed again. "See what I mean?"

By contrast, Chaku hardly ever spoke. He did his duties and at night squatted silently near the fire. Several times Fargo tried to draw him into conversation, but Chaku always answered with a simple yes or no to every question and refused to delve into his personal life.

The seventh evening out, the three of them had eaten and were relaxing. Fargo sipped coffee and savored the rare silence. Emery had been withdrawn the past half hour or so, but Fargo knew it wouldn't last forever. And he was right.

"Ever been in love?"

"If I have, it's not anything I'd share with you."

"It's personal. I savvy. But I didn't mean you. I meant love in general."

"How the hell do you love someone in general?"

"No, no." Emery shook his head. "Let me explain." He rested his elbows on his knees and his chin in his hands. "Growing up, I never had much of an idea what love was all about. Pa married late in life. Real late. Ma was twenty years younger than him." Emery paused and blinked. "I just realized. That's about as old as I am. What do you think of that?"

"Is there a point to this prattle?"

"I don't think Pa married her out of love. I think he married her to have me and my brothers. He wanted heirs. Kids he could leave everything to. He's never told me that's why he married her, but I don't know how else to explain how he treated her."

Despite himself, Fargo asked, "How was that?"

"Pa was always cold to her. Oh, he was polite and all. But you could tell he sort of regarded her as a third arm or leg. She was there but he didn't really need her. Does that make sense?"

"No. But go on."

"Anyway, it always bothered me. She was so pretty and sweet. She never had a harsh word for anyone. I cared for her so much, it hurt. When she hung herself I cried for a week."

"What?"

"Oh. That's right. You didn't know. Yes, she went out to the stable and threw a rope over a beam and stood on a stool and put a noose over her head and then stepped off the stool. I was the one who found her. She was just hanging there, like one of those pendulums in a grandfather clock, swinging back and forth, back and forth, her eyes like glass and the tip of her tongue poking out. It was a sight."

"Why did she take her life?"

"No one rightly knows. She never so much as hinted that she would ever do anything like that. She seemed to be happy, or as happy as she could be. I wish I had known. I'd have stopped her." Emery paused. "Four years ago, it was. Four years ago this month."

"I'm sorry, boy," Fargo said, and meant it. No one deserved to lose a parent like that.

"For a while I didn't much care if I lived or died. Then Evie came along. She had taken up with Adam and he would bring her over, and she was so nice and sweet, just like my ma. I saw that life goes on and I picked myself up and got on with living again."

"That's good," Fargo said, for want of anything else.

"With Adam and Evie I got to see what real love is like. You should have seen them. Always making cow eyes at each other and holding hands and doing for one another. That's real love. Not the love my pa had for my ma. Real love is warm and kind and just about the best thing there is on this earth."

Fargo's respect for the boy rose a notch.

"I want love like that. I want it more than I want anything. If Adam can do it, why not me?"

A few feet away, Chaku raised his head and stared intently at Emery, his face inscrutable.

"You're young yet," Fargo said. "You have plenty of time to find someone."

"I want it now," Emery said.

"It's not always up to us. Love happens when it happens."

Emery looked across the fire. "Then you *have* been in love before?"

"Let's turn in." Fargo drained his cup. He lay on his back with his saddle for a pillow and gazed at the spectacular starry firmament and remembered a particular woman out of the many.

The next day and the day after and the day after that passed without incident. From time to time they came on homesteads and isolated cabins. Once, a big yellow dog came at them barking and snarling and Fargo was about to draw his Colt when a woman came out of the cabin and called the dog off. Another time a man emerged holding a rifle and trained it on them until they were out of range.

"Right friendly cuss," Emery said.

"People living out this far would rather be safe and breathing."

"You ask me, folks worry too much."

They passed the last human habitation. Ahead lay wild country. The dry high prairie gave way to scrub. A gradual rise of the land brought them to the foot of a caprock escarpment that marked the boundary of the Staked Plain. Fargo made camp at the base of the escarpment and set about gathering brush for the fire.

Emery stood with his hands on his hips staring up. "That's it? A kitten could climb that. It's not very high."

"A wagon can't climb." Fargo motioned. "This happens to be one of the best spots for a Conestoga to make it up and over."

"So you brought us this way on purpose."

"It's what your pa is paying for." Fargo bent to pick up a stick, and something caught his eye. "Come take a look."

Emery shuffled over, kicking dust with his boots. "What did you find? A lizard I can stomp?"

Fargo pointed at a rut. "Wagon tracks."

"So?"

"Could be they were made by your brother."

Emery hunkered and placed his hands in it. "You reckon? Then we're smack on their trail. We'll find them in no time."

"Don't get your hopes up," Fargo advised.

"They're alive. I know it. I can feel it in my bones." He turned to Chaku and repeated, "They're alive!"

"Bone is bone," Fargo said.

Their supper consisted of beans. Emery poked at his with his spoon and grumbled, "I'm tired of beans. We have flour and sugar. Why don't you make some biscuits?"

"You don't like what I cook, cook your own meals," Fargo said curtly.

"I'm just saying, is all."

The Ovaro raised its head and nickered. Instantly, Fargo set down his plate, palmed his Colt and backed out of the firelight.

Emery just sat there. "What in God's name are you doing?"

From out of the dark in the direction of the slope up to the escarpment came a shout. "Hello, the fire! We'd like to come and sit a spell, my brother and me, if you're agreeable."

Jumping up, Emery nearly spilled his food. "Who's that?" he hollered.

"Who's out there?"

Chaku didn't move or speak.

"We're friendly," the voice assured them.

Fargo cupped a hand to his mouth. "Come on down. We have coffee if you want some." He stayed where he was.

Pebbles rattled, and out of the murk appeared two men leading horses. One was heavyset and grubby, the other rake thin. Both had stubble covering their chins. The heavyset man wore a bulky coat in need of mending even though it was summer. Neither had a holster or was carrying a rifle. Heavyset had a floppy hat; the other had no hat at all. They were leading their horses by the reins.

Heavyset introduced them. "Howdy. My name is Lem. This here is my brother, Clovis. That coffee you have on sure smells good."

"You're welcome to have a cup," Emery said.

"That's hospitable of you, boy," Lem said. He looked around. "Wasn't there someone else? I thought I counted three."

Fargo unfurled and stepped into the light with the Colt leveled. "That would be me."

Lem and Clovis turned and Lem said, "Hold on there, mister. No need for the hardware."

Emery was as surprised as they were. "Why do you have your six-shooter out? They've made it plain they're not out to hurt us."

"Have they?" Fargo said.

Lem licked his thick lips. "We called out to you, didn't we? When we could just as well have shot you from off in the dark without you knowing we were even there."

Clovis held his arms out from his sides. "All we want is some coffee, mister. We ran out a while back and we'd be powerful happy if you'd see fit to share."

"Have a seat," Fargo said. He waited until they did; then he holstered the Colt and moved around the fire so he was across from them. Squatting, he folded his arms across his legs. "A man can't be too careful," he said, justifying his conduct.

"True enough," Lem said. "Them that ain't are more likely to lose their hair, or worse."

Emery sat back down and put his plate in his lap. "What are you two doing so far from anywhere, if you don't mind my asking?"

"We're on our way to New Orleans," Lem revealed. "Got us a cousin there who says we can make good money working on the waterfront."

"Hard workers, are you?" Fargo asked.

"A man fills his belly how he can," Lem said. "We came west from Missouri back in 'forty-nine thinking we would strike it rich, but we never found enough gold to fill a poke. Stayed on, though, because we liked the country."

"But now we're tired of wandering," Clovis said. "We'd like to settle down with a regular job. When our cousin wrote us, we decided to take him up on it."

"How about that coffee?" Lem said eagerly. "We have our own cups to drink out of."

"Help yourselves," Emery said.

Fargo watched closely as Lem went to their horses and rummaged in their saddlebags and came back holding two badly dented and scratched tin cups. Lem gave one to Clovis and poured for the both of them.

Lem cradled his cup in his hands, took a sip and let out with a loud "Ahhhh. We're obliged. It's been so long, I had about forgot how good coffee tastes."

"Seen any sign of a wagon hereabouts?" Fargo asked.

Emery was quick to say, "A Conestoga. Belongs to my brother and his wife. Adam and Evie Broxton."

Lem and Clovis swapped looks and Lem said, "Can't say as we have."

"That's too bad," Emery said.

"What is a wagon doing out this far?" Lem asked, and nodded at the escarpment. "Up yonder is the Staked Plain. Hundreds of miles of god-awful hell fit for neither man nor beast. Why would anyone bring their missus and a wagon here?"

"They were on their way to Santa Fe."

Clovis snorted in amusement. "Across the Staked Plain? Is your brother loco? He'll only get him and his woman killed."

"Don't say that," Emery said harshly.

"Do you have any idea what's up there, boy?" Lem asked. "Any idea at all?"

"I do," Fargo said.

The brothers looked at him and Lem said, "Yes, you would. I'm a good judge of men and you have more bark on you than most."

For a while the only sounds were the crackling of the fire and sipping noises and then Lem turned to Emery. "Listen, boy. Out here ain't like the world you're used to. Out here it's every coon for himself. Those that are puny and those that are green don't last. You got upset with me, but I was only saying how it is. Ask your friend here if you don't believe me."

"He said the same thing you have," Emery said. "But we've come this far without a lick of trouble and the first people we meet are you two and you're friendly enough."

"We made it a point to be," Lem said.

"You catch more flies with honey, boy, than you do with dirt," Clovis remarked.

"Plus we like to get in close," Lem said.

Emery glanced from one to the other in confusion. "What does honey and dirt have to do with anything?"

Fargo started to lower his right hand to his holster.

"I wouldn't," Lem said. "There's four of us, not two. We've done our part and kept you talking. A gent named Balsam is behind you and our pard Walt is behind the black and they are both fond of spilling blood."

Metallic clicks confirmed the threat, but Fargo looked behind him anyway, into the muzzle of a Starr revolver.

Chaku didn't move or even blink. He didn't act the least bit rattled.

Emery half rose but Lem shoved him back down. "What is this? What are you up to?"

"Dumb as a turnip," Clovis said.

"I am not!"

Lem smiled a cold smile. "You're so dumb, you don't know you're dumb. We aim to rob you, boy. To take your horses and your money and your guns and leave you for the buzzards." Lem's smile widened. "After we've had our fun."

5

Balsam and Walt came around in front of Fargo and Chaku. All four were grinning at how cleverly their ruse had worked. Lem reached under his coat and produced a Smith & Wesson. "You must be feeling awful stupid yourself right about now."

"I have my moments," Fargo said.

Lem chuckled. "You remind me a bit of Santos. Too bad I have to put windows in your skull."

"Who?"

"The head of our band. That wagon you're searching for? He can tell you right where it is." Lem and Clovis laughed.

"Wait a minute," Emery said in confusion. "Band of what? Are you outlaws?"

"Some might call us that," Lem replied.

Clovis said, "Most call us Comancheros."

"Comancheros?" Emery repeated. "Aren't they the ones who sell rifles and knives and the like to the Comanches?"

"That's us, boy" Lem said. "And Comancheros like to play with their prey first."

"How is it you were waiting for us?" Emery asked.

"Not you, boy. Anyone who came along. Santos sends us out in small groups to look for jackasses who should know better than to come to the Staked Plain country."

Clovis nodded. "White, Mex, it's no difference to us. We kill anybody and everybody and take what we want."

The man called Walt was standing near Chaku. "What's with this darkie? Why is he dressed like an Apache?"

The Katonza was wearing the long loincloth that Fargo had seen him wear that night in the garden behind the mansion. It was his only attire.

"He's from Africa," Emery said.

"Who the hell cares?" Clovis threw in.

Lem went over and studied the huge black. "Strange cuss, ain't you? Can you talk or did someone cut out your tongue?"

"I talk," Chaku said.

Lem bent and picked up an object at the Katonza's feet. "What the hell is this? A walking stick?"

Fargo had been puzzled, too, when he first saw it. Chaku called it a *knojbe*. Emery told Fargo that Chaku had carved it himself from hardwood. It consisted of a handle or shaft about two feet long with a large knob or ball at one end. Fargo had asked Chaku why he made it. Chaku answered that it was a favorite weapon of his people.

Lem wagged the club and chortled. "A big mountain of muscle like you carries a puny thing like this? You'd be better off wearing iron."

Chaku might have been a statue.

"You'll talk to me, I promise you," Lem said, and threw the club aside.

"Let's shoot him and be done with it," Clovis suggested. "He doesn't have anything we can use."

"I'm thinking we tie the three of them and have fun with them in the morning," Lem said. "Maybe strip them and set them free and hunt them down like we did those Quakers."

"Why wait?"

"Because I say to." Lem stepped over to Fargo and snatched the Colt from his holster. "You won't be needing this."

Fargo was furious with himself. He had suspected they were up to no good and been on his guard, but he hadn't reckoned on there being two more. Mistakes like that were the reason the Staked Plain was dotted with sun-bleached bones.

"You don't seem none too happy," Lem taunted. "Look at the bright side of things."

"There *is* a bright side?"

"You're still breathing. If I was Santos, you'd have a bullet in your brain by now."

"Why so considerate?"

"Haven't you been paying attention? Where's the fun in killing you outright?"

"You keep using that word."

"Fun?" Lem chuckled. "I like having a good time. Whiskey, women, killing, it's all the same to me."

"Quit gabbing and tie them," Clovis said. "They're dangerous until they're trussed up."

"Not with the four of us covering them, they ain't." Lem motioned at Balsam. "Fetch a rope. Then you and Walt tend to it."

Fargo smothered an impulse to resist. Now wasn't the time. He let Balsam jerk his arms behind him and loop a length of rope tight. Chaku didn't resist, either. Then it was Emery's turn. The instant that Balsam grabbed hold of his wrist, Emery shoved him.

"Stay away from me! I won't let you, you hear?"

"Calm down, boy," Lem said. "You don't want to rile us."

"How can I stay calm when you're out to kill us?"

"I'm warning you."

"Don't do this," Emery said. "We don't have much. Just our horses and supplies and guns. But if you spare us, I'll see to it that you get a lot more than they are worth."

"How would you work that?" Lem asked.

"My pa has money. Lots of money. Leave us be and I'll have him pay each of you a thousand dollars. Honest I will."

"We let you go," Lem scoffed, "we'll never see hide nor hair of you or any money."

"Please," Emery pleaded. "I have to find my brother. I have to find his wife. It means everything to me."

"How nice. But you see, boy, me and my friends don't give a damn." At that, Lem threw back his head and roared with mirth. He was still laughing when Emery reached up under his sleeve, drew a derringer, and shot Lem between the eyes.

Rooted in disbelief, the other three Comancheros watched as Lem melted to the ground like so much porridge.

Fargo was as stunned as everyone else. He didn't know the boy had a hide-out.

Clovis recovered enough to roar in rage. "No!"

Emery bolted. All three remaining Comancheros started after him, but Clovis snarled at Balsam and Walt to stay put and lit out into the darkness after his brother's slayer.

Balsam stood over Lem and said, "Damn, damn, damn. Why didn't one of us check that boy?"

"Santos will have a fit," Walt said. "He doesn't like it when any of us is careless."

"Lem and his gab, anyhow," Balsam complained. "He always did flap his gums too damn much."

"Kill first, talk later, I always say," Walt said.

Fargo shifted his leg and slid his fingers into his boot. He was about to slide the Arkansas toothpick out when Balsam turned toward him.

"I wouldn't want to be you, mister, when Clovis gets back. He'll be powerful mad about his brother dying, and when he gets mad, he gets ugly."

Walt nodded. "He's liable to skin you alive. He did that once to a parson we caught. Skinned him and cut off his nose and his ears and staked him out in the hot sun until he died."

"The whole time, all that parson did was pray," Balsam said. "He didn't scream. He didn't beg. He just prayed."

"Not that it did him any good," Walt said.

They turned and gazed off into the night.

Fargo set to work. He slid the toothpick from his boot, reversed his grip and sliced. Across the fire, Chaku's shoulders were moving up and down, but Fargo couldn't tell what the Katonza was doing.

"It's awful quiet out there," Walt said to his companion. "Do you reckon one of us should go see if Clovis is all right?"

"He told us to stay put and that's what I'm doing. He can take care of himself."

"Lem could take care of himself, too, and look at where it got him. That boy is a tricky cuss."

"Shot by a green kid," Balsam said. "Lem deserved better."

Fargo strained. The rope was parting but not fast enough. Any moment the pair would turn and he would lose his chance. Gritting his teeth from the pain in his wrists, he continued to cut.

Chaku stopped moving his shoulders. He looked at the two Comancheros and then at Fargo and moved his hands from behind him so Fargo could see that he was free. Soundlessly, Chaku rose into a crouch and crept toward his club.

Bunching his arms, Fargo exerted all his strength and the remaining strands snapped. Holding the toothpick at his waist, he stalked toward the two Comancheros.

Chaku had his club and was doing the same.

"We could yell to Clovis and ask if he is all right," Walt was saying.

"And have him answer and the kid knows right where he is?" Balsam shook his head.

"We should take the kid to Santos. Santos will carve him up good for killing Lem."

"You think Clovis won't?"

By then Fargo was close enough. He glanced at Chaku and nodded and together they sprang. Fargo hooked his left forearm around Balsam's throat even as he sank the toothpick to the hilt below the man's right shoulder blade. Balsam didn't scream; he didn't struggle. He simply went limp, exhaled once and that was it.

Wet drops spattered Fargo's cheek.

Walt was folding with half his head caved in. Chaku loomed over him, blood dripping from the ball at the end of the Katonza's club.

Fargo yanked the toothpick out and wiped the blade clean on Balsam's shirt. Reclaiming his Colt, he replaced the knife in his ankle sheath. "I'm going to find Emery. You coming?"

The warrior grunted.

"Is that a yes or a no?"

Chaku pointed.

Emery was walking toward them. Or, rather, he was *strolling* toward them as if he didn't have a care in the world. "I saw what you did to those two," he said. "Good riddance."

"There's still the other one, Clovis," Fargo said. "We have to find him and deal with him. If he gets away he'll bring other Comancheros."

"He's not going anywhere," Emery said.

"How do you know?"

"He's dead."

"Dead how?" Fargo asked in some amazement.

"How do you think?" Emery rejoined. He squatted and picked up his tin cup. "He came after me and I killed him like I killed his brother. They weren't very smart, either of them."

Fargo absorbed what the younger man was saying. "Comancheros don't die easy. How did you kill Clovis? I didn't hear a shot."

Emery sipped his coffee and smacked his lips. "I snuck up on him and beaned him with a rock."

First the derringer, now this. Fargo's notions about the boy were proving to be all wrong. In fact, Fargo decided to stop thinking of him as a *boy* and more as a *man*, and a deadly little man, at that. "You surprise me," he admitted.

"Folks say that all the time. They think I am next to useless, but there are some things I do well. Like killing."

"Are you saying you've killed before?"

Emery nodded.

Surprise piled on surprise. Fargo studied him, seeking to fathom how he could have been so wrong. "I would never have guessed," he remarked, hoping Emery would tell him more.

"I reckon I don't look that tough, do I?" Emery chuckled. "I hide it real well, like I hide most things about me."

"Such as?"

Emery shrugged. "This and that."

Chaku was imitating a statue again. Fargo looked at him and their eyes met and it seemed the Katonza's features changed in some slight manner that Fargo could not quite read.

"I told you I could take care of myself and I meant it," Emery was elaborating. "Comancheros didn't scare me none. Neither do Comanches or Apaches or outlaws."

"No one likes a braggart," Fargo said.

"It's not bragging when it's a fact."

"You're too full of yourself."

"Am I? I had no trouble killing those two. But then, it's always come easy to me. When it needs doing I do it, and that's that."

"You should have told me this sooner."

"I didn't think it was important."

"What is?"

Emery smiled enigmatically. "That's for me to know and you to find out, if you can."

Fargo didn't know what to make of him. He truly didn't. "Why did your father send Chaku along to protect you when you don't need protecting?"

"Pa didn't say but I can pretty much guess. He didn't send Chaku to protect me from others." Emery drained his cup and let out an "Ahhhhh." Gripping the coffeepot, he commenced to refill it. "Pa sent Chaku to protect others from me."

6

Fargo had a lot to think about over the next several days. He couldn't quite make up his mind about Emery Broxton. Was Emery a natural-born killer or was he boasting when he talked about having killed before?

The trail led up the escarpment and on into the dark heart of the Staked Plain. Now and then they came upon wagon ruts that led in the same direction. The marks were so faint and so old it was impossible to say if they had been made by Adam and Evie's Conestoga, but Fargo considered it likely.

Chaku was his usual quiet self. He didn't talk about the other night, except once. They had stopped at midday to rest the horses. Chaku was holding his club.

Fargo nodded at it and said, "That brain crusher of yours is some weapon. You smashed that bastard's skull in."

Chaku placed his big hand on the heavy ball and rubbed it as if he were stroking a cat. "Clubs good weapon, yes. Katonga use them. Katonza use *lankuisi*. Katonga use *lankuasa*."

"I don't know what they are."

"*Lankuisi* long spear. *Lankuasa* is short spear."

"Two spears?"

"Long spear for throw and short spear for stab. I like stab."

"Your people must do a lot of fighting." Fargo was thinking of how certain Indian tribes were constantly at war with one another. The Shoshones and the Sioux. The Apaches and the Pimas. The Blackfeet and just about everybody.

"We fight much," Chaku confirmed. "We have many enemies." A suggestion of a grin touched his mouth. "White men are our enemies." He wagged his club. "White heads smash nice."

"Do you have a family back in Katonzaland?"

Chaku's face clouded. "Had family. Arabs shoot wife when she try help me. I see her die."

There was nothing that Fargo could say beyond "I'm sorry to hear that."

"Arabs take our children," Chaku said sadly. "I not know where they are."

"They use children as slaves, too?"

"They take everyone they not kill."

Fargo was troubled. He hadn't realized the extent of the slave trade until now. Without thinking he asked, "Is Rohesia a Katonza?"

"No."

"Good thing you met her," Fargo said. He figured as how it might help a little to ease the warrior's pain.

Chaku got up and walked off.

"What did I say?" Fargo wondered out loud, and from behind him there was a chuckle.

"Don't take it personal, scout," Emery said, coming up. "My pa says that Katonzas aren't like most slaves. They don't mingle much. And they sure as hell don't like whites."

"A slave who doesn't like his masters. Hard to imagine."

Emery cocked his head. "You jab people a lot—do you know that?"

"Just so I don't leave bruises."

"And when you're not jabbing, you spout nonsense. What the hell did that just mean?"

"You'd have to ask my horse."

"Ask your . . ." Emery stopped and tapped his temple. "It must be the sun. Folks say that if you're out in it too much, it can fry the brain."

"Are you out in it much?"

"Me? No more than I have to be. Why would I be out in the hot sun when I live in a mansion that stays cool most of the day?"

"It's a wonderment," Fargo said.

"There is only so much of you I can take," Emery informed him, and walked off.

"I must need a bath," Fargo said.

On the fifth morning they came on a wide swath of pock-marked earth where a large body of riders had passed. Fargo dismounted and sank to one knee to study the prints.

"More Comancheros?" Emery asked.

"Indians. The horses weren't shod." Fargo tried to count them but it was impossible. "Sixty or more. Comanches, would be my guess."

"A war party, you reckon?"

"Hunting parties aren't usually this big. It must be a war party on its way to raid along the border. Or maybe push clear into Mexico."

"Sixty," Emery said. "We wouldn't stand much of a chance against that many."

"We wouldn't stand any chance at all."

More days went by. Days of relentless sun and sweat and flies. They were in the heart of the Staked Plain, where few whites had ever been. Rugged land. Harsh land.

There came an afternoon when they were skirting a gorge and Emery rose in his stirrups to stare down into it. "What in the world was my brother thinking? Dragging his wife out here? No one could get a wagon across this hell."

"I told you that back at the mansion," Fargo reminded him.

"I still feel they are alive," Emery said defensively.

"In your bones?"

"Don't start. I am hot and prickly and not in the mood for your barbs." Emery took off his hat and ran his sleeve across his brow. "I wish it would rain."

"You don't mean that."

43

"Why don't I?"

"Because the rain would wipe out the tracks and any chance we have of finding this Santos and maybe learning what happened to Adam and Evie."

"Oh. Well, I wish it would cool down some, then."

"Wait about six months. They call it winter."

"My pa was right. You're a regular wiseacre."

Hills rose, stark and barren. A patch of green suggested a spring. While the Ovaro drank, Fargo roved about reading sign. Hoofprints were everywhere. Horses shod and horses not shod. Most of the shod tracks either came from or headed to the northwest.

From then on Fargo rode with the Henry across his saddle. A day and a half brought them to a low ridge that overlooked the entrance to a canyon. High rock walls hid whatever was beyond.

"Stay with the horses," Fargo told Emery and Chaku. "I'm going to have a look-see."

"Why can't I go?" Emery wanted to know. "I can be as sneaky as anyone. Lem found that out the hard way."

"One man has less chance of being spotted." To nip an argument, Fargo glided down the rise, moving from boulder to boulder. At the bottom was a convenient patch of dry brush. Dropping onto his belly, he crawled to where he could see the canyon mouth. He expected to find sentries, but there were none.

Fargo settled in to wait. There was no hurry. After the pair had been missing for so many weeks, a few more hours wouldn't matter. Either Adam and Evie were alive or they weren't.

Hardly two minutes went by and several riders came out of the canyon. One wore a sombrero, another an old beaver hat. All wore armories. They were talking and smiling. At ease, as they should be, since no one had ever penetrated this near to their lair. They rode off to the east.

The sun broiled Fargo's back. Beads of sweat trickled from under his hat.

He would dearly love to wipe it off, but he stayed as motionless as a rock. He was like an Apache in that respect; he could keep perfectly still for hours if he had to.

After a while two more riders came out. They, too, wore sombreros. They trotted north, raising swirls of dust.

The sun was on its downward arc. Another couple of hours and it would set, shrouding the Staked Plain in twilight.

Something brushed against Fargo's elbow. Startled, he looked, thinking it might be a snake or some other animal.

"I didn't mean to spook you," Emery Broxton whispered.

Fargo hid his shock. No one could get so close to him without him noticing. Not even an Apache. Yet this snip of a greenhorn had somehow done just that. "I told you to stay put."

"I was bored waiting," Emery complained. "Chaku is watching the horses, if that's what you're worried about."

"Go back. I'll be along."

"Like hell you will. You aim to sneak on in there, don't you?"

"I shouldn't be more than an hour. Any more than that and it means they've caught me. You and Chaku should light a shuck."

"I'm not leaving until I know if the Comancheros had anything to do with Evie and Adam."

"If I see a Conestoga I'll let you know," Fargo said.

"No need. I'm going with you."

"You think you are."

Emery laughed. "You can't stop me short of shooting me and the shot would bring the Comancheros."

Fargo wanted to hit him. It was risk enough for one man. They had forty yards of open ground to cover and no way of knowing what they would find once they were in the canyon. "I'd take it as a personal favor if you would stay here."

"Don't you talk pretty?" Emery said, and chortled. "But I'm going and that's all there is to it."

The smart thing was to wait until dark, but the dark would hinder as well as help, and Fargo opted not to wait. He was up and running in a burst of speed. Emery stayed at his side, a surprise in itself given that Fargo was considered fleet of foot.

High walls framed ground that sloped to a sharp bend. Fargo listened, and when he didn't hear voices or hoofbeats, he peered around. He wasn't sure exactly what to expect, but he sure didn't expect what he saw.

The canyon floor widened to half a mile at its broadest and was a little less than a mile from end to end. From under a cliff at the far end flowed a ribbon of water that meandered down the middle. The water flowed under a rock spur at the near end and didn't reappear.

Thanks to the water the canyon was a Garden of Eden, an oasis of green in a desert of mostly baked brown. Oaks and willows lined the stream and grew in stands at scattered points. Grass enough for a herd of hundreds was being grazed by a few dozen head of cattle and fifty or sixty horses.

About midway in stood a cluster of cabins and lean-tos and an honest-to-God house with a large black pot on a tripod in front. Horses were tied to hitch rails, saddled and ready to ride. Dogs roamed at will. And there were people, plenty of people, moving about or lounging in the shade. More than a few were women.

"I'll be switched," Emery said.

Fargo had heard tell that Comanchero bands had secret havens deep in the Staked Plain, but he never reckoned on anything like this. It was as if a small settlement had been plopped down in the middle of the most godforsaken spot in creation.

Emery gripped Fargo's arm and pointed. "Look there. Yonder past the last building, under those trees. Do you see what I see?"

Fargo did: a Conestoga, dappled by shadow. The canvas had been ripped and flapped in the breeze. Nearby were a pair of freight wagons, probably used by the Comancheros to transport trade goods to the Comanches.

Emery went to go past. "Out of my way. That's their wagon. I'd know it anywhere."

Grabbing his wrist, Fargo held fast. "Think, damn it. Run out there in the open and you'll get yourself killed. You can't do them any good dead." Provided they were still alive.

"It's just that after coming all this way I want to see . . ." Emery took a few deep breaths to calm himself. "Sorry. I'm not thinking straight."

"We take it slow and we live longer."

"Understood. What do you want me to do?"

"Stay close." Fargo flattened and snaked to a thicket. Once around it, he rose but stayed low.

Emery was behind him. "What now? Work our way around to the wagons?"

Fargo nodded. There was ample cover. The lack of guards helped, too.

Some of the Comancheros were white, some were Mexicans, a few were Indians. Fully half appeared to be a mix. Halfbreeds, they were called. Their clothes reflected their diversity. All the men and some of the women were armed. A lot of rifles were in evidence. Most of those moving about were not busy at any particular task. They appeared to be taking it easy, waiting for the worst of the day's heat to fade.

The house interested Fargo. It was poorly constructed, but that it had been built at all was a marvel. Comancheros were not noted for being industrious except when there was money to be made. It hinted that whoever lived in it must be someone high in the Comanchero band.

"I don't see Evie or Adam anywhere," Emery whispered.

"Patience," Fargo cautioned.

"If you only knew," Emery said, but he did not say what it was Fargo should know.

They were across from the buildings when a young woman of Spanish descent, with lustrous hair flowing to her waist, emerged from a cabin and unexpectedly came toward them. Instantly Fargo flattened, pulling Emery with him. Emery started to say something but Fargo put a finger to his lips and nodded at the woman.

Fargo doubted she had seen them. They were in high grass amid trees. He was perplexed when she kept coming and then he saw the reason.

A few feet away grew a patch of yellow and purple wildflowers. The woman was making straight for the patch.

She was bound to spot them.

7

Skye Fargo drew his Colt. He didn't want to harm the woman if he could help it, but he couldn't let her cry out. Her shout would bring a swarm of Comancheros.

"Want me to kill her?" Emery whispered. He had a knife in his hand and was grinning in anticipation.

"No."

"She'll see us."

"Let me handle her."

"Are you sure you can?"

By then the woman was close enough. Fargo coiled his legs, primed to spring. He noticed how beautiful she was: a lovely oval face, full cheeks and full lips and a sway to her hips that would make most any man hungry. Her cotton dress accented the swell of her full bosom and the shapely contours of her thighs.

A lark drew her attention. So did a butterfly. She was almost to the wildflowers when she glanced over her shoulder at the cabins.

Fargo made his move. He was up and on her in three long bounds. Jamming the Colt against her stomach, he warned, "Not a sound."

The lovely regarded him with astounding calm. Her dark eyes gleamed with what Fargo swore was amusement as she quietly said, "Eeeek."

"I meant it."

"Shoot me, senor, and you will have over forty of my

friends down on you. Can you fight that many? I think not."
Her eyes flicked from his head to his boots and back again.
"And it would be a shame for someone so handsome to be
shot to pieces."

"I'd rather not shoot you or your friends if I can help it."

"They will not feel the same. To them, all strangers are to
be robbed and killed."

"And you?"

"Me, senor? My father is a Comanchero, so I was born to
this life. But I am not so fond of the robbing and the killing.
Red is not my favorite color."

Fargo liked her. "How do they call you?"

"I am Ria, senor. Ria Gonzales." She grinned and imp-
ishly said, "Well, senor? Are you going to stand here all day
with your *pistola* in my navel? Someone is bound to see you."

"Come with me." Fargo pulled her past the wildflowers
and over behind a willow. He lowered the Colt but didn't holster it. To trust her would be reckless. "I need information."

"I am nineteen, senor. I like handsome men. I like them
very much." Ria looked him up and down some more. "What
name did your *madre* give someone so handsome?"

Fargo tore his eyes from her abundant bosom and told
her, his voice not sounding like him.

"Sky as in above us?" Ria said, and pointed up.

Fargo spelled it for her.

"S-k-y-e." She rolled each letter on her tongue as if it were
hard candy. "An unusual name. What is it you would like to
know?"

Before Fargo could ask her a question, Emery was there,
wagging his knife, his lips curled like a wolf about to pounce.

"What are you waiting for? Kill her and be done with it."

Ria regarded him with distaste. "Who is this, senor? He
does not have your manners or your charm."

Emery started to lunge at her, but Fargo stepped between
them and put a hand on Emery's chest.

"You're not to harm her, you hear?"

"What the hell? She's one of them." Emery raised the knife and tried to get past.

Fargo pointed the Colt at him. "I say what I mean and mean what I say. Hurt her and you won't like what comes next."

"This is a hell of a note," Emery grumbled, but he lowered his knife and stepped back. "I don't understand you sometimes."

Fargo turned to Ria.

"Thank you, senor. Your young friend is impetuous. Why does he want to kill me so much?"

Fargo looked away. Her beauty was intoxicating. Standing so close, he was growing warm all over. He reminded himself why he was there and focused on that and only that. Or tried to. "The Conestoga over yonder."

"What about it, Skye?"

The way she said his name, so sultry and inviting, made Fargo tingle.

"It belongs to his brother and sister-in-law. We're here to find out what happened to them."

"Ah," Ria said. She smiled at Emery. "I forgive you, then."

"Forgive me for what, you damned Mex?" was his retort. "Did I ask for your forgiveness? Tell us what we want to know, or Fargo or not, I'll stick you and keep sticking you until you do."

"Red is your favorite color, I see."

"No, it's not. My favorite color is orange. Not that it's any of your business. Why the hell are we talking colors, anyway?"

"I do not like you," Ria said.

Emery glowered and took half a step but glanced at Fargo and stopped. "And I don't like you, bitch. So we're even."

"Enough," Fargo said, and focused on Ria. "What can you tell us about the wagon and the couple who own it?"

"They are alive and well. Or well enough."

"Did you hear her?" Emery exclaimed, much too loudly. "Evie and Adam are alive!" He excitedly gripped Fargo's arm. "I told you, didn't I? I told you I could feel it in my bones."

Fargo shrugged loose. "What else?" he said to Ria.

"They were very foolish. They tried to cross the Llano Estacado. Some of our men came on their tracks and caught them and brought them here." Ria paused. "Two weeks ago, it was, or maybe a little longer. They have been here since."

"I'm so happy I could bust," Emery declared.

Fargo was thinking that it was rare for Comancheros to be so merciful. "Why haven't your people killed them?"

"The men never kill women if the women are pretty, and the yellow-haired one is very pretty."

"Evie," Emery said. "Her name is Evie."

"I know. Her husband called himself Adam, but Santos, our leader, has given him a new name."

"What are you talking about?"

"Your brother is now called Dog."

"I should punch you in the mouth."

Fargo poked him, hard. "Simmer down, damn you. She can't tell us if you keep interrupting."

Ria bestowed a radiant smile on him. "Thank you. Permit me to explain."

She seemed to become slightly sad. "When they and their wagon were brought here, Santos said anyone could have the woman who wanted her. Wilson took her. He is ugly and mean and very quick on the trigger, and he is second to Santos."

Emery had gone pale. "What do you mean, he took her? Took Evie how?"

"How do you think?" Ria rejoined. "Wilson took her to his cabin and she has been there since. She is allowed out now and then, but she is hobbled so she can not run away."

"He *took* her," Emery said, and his whole body trembled.

"What about the husband?" Fargo prompted.

"Santos took Adam for himself. Which was strange since

Adam is white and Santos hates whites except those who ride for him. Although I suspect he secretly hates even them."

"Santos took Adam?" Emery said.

"He is a cat, that one. He likes to play with his prey. Sometimes he ties them to a post at the back of his house and feeds them scraps to keep them alive so he can beat them and kick them when it pleases him. This Adam he treats different."

"Different how?" Fargo asked.

"The first day, Santos began to beat him and Adam groveled and cried and begged him not to. I could not look, I was so ashamed for his weakness. Santos stopped beating him and gripped his hair and laughed. 'You are a yellow dog, gringo,' he said. 'That is what we will call you. Dog. From here on you are my dog and you will do as I say, when I say.'"

"The bastard," Emery breathed.

"Santos put a leash on Adam and treats him just as if he were a real dog. He walks him and pets him and has him beg for food."

Emery was shaking with fury.

"I do not like it but there is nothing I can do," Ria said. "There is much my people do that I do not like."

"Why stay, then?" Fargo wondered.

"I told you. My father is a Comanchero. It is all he will ever be. My mother stays because she loves him and I stay because I love the both of them."

Fargo thought he heard voices and risked a quick look around the willow.

Two men were over at the wagons, talking. He ducked back. "Will you help us free Adam and his wife?"

Without hesitation Ria said, "No."

Emery bristled. "Why not? You just said you don't agree with what your people do."

"I do not like to steal or kill, *sí*. But they are still my people. I am a Comanchero. I will not betray them."

"It would make it easier for us," Fargo mentioned. "No one need be hurt."

"I cannot."

Emery angrily thrust his knife at Fargo but stopped short of stabbing him. "You see? She'll warn them if we let her go. You should let me stick her so she can't."

"I will not tell anyone about you," Ria said.

"You expect us to believe that? You're one of them, for God's sake. You'll warn them to spare them and we'll wind up dead."

Ria appealed to Fargo. "He is wrong. I'll give you my word if you will give me yours that my father and my mother will not be harmed."

"How will we know it's them if there is shooting?" Fargo brought up.

"I have an idea. But I want your word first."

"We'll try our best not to kill anyone at all," Fargo promised.

"Hell," Emery said.

"Very well. Here is my idea. We always eat supper together. All of us. The food is cooked in a big pot in front of—"

"I saw it," Fargo broke in.

"Good. Then you know where it is. We eat and drink and relax. Often we stay up late. That is when you should try for her. Wilson rarely brings your Evie to supper. Santos sometimes has Adam with him but only to have Adam beg and roll over and do dog tricks."

"The bastard," Emery said.

"You're saying we could sneak in and get them and slip off with no one the wiser," Fargo concluded.

"It is your best chance, yes. But you must be careful. Watch out for the real dogs. They might bark and give you away."

"I don't trust her," Emery said to Fargo.

"I do."

"Thank you," Ria said. She bobbed her chin at the sun,

54

which was low on the horizon. "It is only an hour until we eat. Hide here and wait for the right moment." She turned to go.

"No so fast." Emery seized her wrist. "We'll do as you want but you're staying with us."

"I will be missed."

"Let her go," Fargo said.

Emery puffed up his chest like an angry rooster. "This is a mistake. The worst we could make."

"Let her go," Fargo said again.

"Fine." Cursing under his breath, Emery pushed her. "Get the hell out of here. And so help me, if you give us away, I'll kill you if it's the last thing on this earth I do."

Ria ignored him and smiled at Fargo. "Another time, another place, eh, handsome one?"

"Another time, another place," Fargo agreed. He watched her sway off and stirred below his belt. Backing from the willow, he skirted the dense thicket and hunkered. "Here will do to wait."

Emery squatted and twitched as if he had ants under his clothes. "I don't like this. I don't like it one bit."

"You've made that plain."

"How can you trust her?"

"I feel it in my bones," Fargo said with a grin.

"You must have your brains in your pants."

"Careful."

"It's stupid, I tell you. She's laughing at us even as we talk. She'll tell them about us and we'll walk into a trap. You wait and see if we don't."

"Could be," Fargo allowed. "We have to try."

"So you say. But I want you to know something. If you're wrong about her, if she turns on us and we're caught, I will by God hold it against you."

"I'm obliged for the warning."

"Go ahead. Mock me. That jackass Lem mocked me and where is he now?" Emery swore anew.

"You need to learn to take things easy."

"Go to hell. I may not know a lot, but there is one thing I do know."

"What would that be?" Fargo asked when he didn't go on.

"No one mocks me and lives."

8

Sunset was spectacular. The sky was lit with bright red, orange and yellow.

Gradually the gray of twilight mantled the Staked Plain. In the canyon it grew darker quickly.

A fire was kindled. Water was poured into the cooking pot. Women cut up potatoes and carrots and dropped the pieces in. Other women butchered an antelope that a Comanchero had brought back and added the dripping chunks of red meat.

By then nearly all of them were there. From every cabin and lean-to they came, hard men and their women. Liquor was passed around and it wasn't long before everyone was talking and smiling.

One Comanchero in particular drew Fargo's interest. A white man. He was big and broad and carried himself with arrogance. A scar ran from under his right eye to his chin. He had a bulbous nose and beady eyes and wore two pistols.

From the way he barked orders and everyone made way for him, Fargo reckoned it must be Wilson, the second-in-command.

The last Comanchero to appear came from the house. One look and Fargo recognized as deadly a human rattler as he ever came across. Of Mexican lineage, the late arrival wore the flashiest clothes, including large silver spurs and silver conchos on a wide leather belt. A pearl-handled Remington adorned his hip. But it was the stamp of cruelty on the man's face that impressed Fargo most. Savagery glittered in those dark eyes and was mirrored in the slash of his mouth.

"That must be Santos," Fargo whispered.

Santos wasn't alone. He was holding a leash. At the end of it, moving on all fours, was a wreck of a white man.

"Adam!" Emery would have risen from their hiding place had Fargo not grabbed him and pulled him back down.

"Stay put. It's not time yet."

Adam Broxton was thin as a rail. His clothes were filthy, his shirt in tatters. He was barefoot, his feet in terrible shape. His hair was a mess and filthy and stuck out like wire.

Santos brought his human dog over to the fire. Some of the others laughed.

Wilson drew back a leg to kick Adam but Santos said something and Wilson lowered the leg again. Santos then addressed a woman who used a large wooden spoon to ladle a small piece of undercooked meat from the pot and dropped it in the dirt in front of the human dog.

The sight of Adam Broxton pathetically tearing at the meat with quaking fingers balled Fargo's gut into a knot. He made a vow then and there, a vow he kept to himself.

Emery's chin drooped to his chest and he groaned.

"Be strong," Fargo whispered. "We'll get them out."

"What sort of animals are they? How can they do such a thing?"

"There's no lack of people who like to hurt other people in this world," Fargo observed.

When Emery raised his head, his face was a mask of rage. "If it's the last thing I ever do, I'll make that Santos pay."

"Get in line," Fargo said. "The important thing is to get your brother and his wife out. We do that before we do anything else."

"Sweet, wonderful Evie." Emery pointed at Wilson. "Do

you think that's the one the Mex woman told us about? The one who claimed her?"

Fargo nodded.

"He's going to die, too."

"A while ago you wanted to kill me," Fargo reminded him.

"Santos and Wilson come first."

"No. Adam and his wife come first. Remember that."

Laughter rose from the camp. Santos was having Adam do tricks. Santos had him squat on his hind legs and whine for another piece of meat, then had him roll over.

"Goddamn that bastard," Emery boiled. "Goddamn him to hell."

Santos made Adam jump up and down on all fours, then patted him as a man might a pet. One of the other Comancheros voiced a comment that had everyone chuckling and grinning.

"They are pure evil," Emery said.

Fargo saw Ria with a gray-haired Comanchero and an older woman. Her parents, he guessed.

"How much longer?" Emery impatiently asked.

"It depends on Santos."

Ria had told them that Santos never kept Adam at the fire for very long, and sure enough, Santos tugged on the leash and took Adam back to the house and on around behind it. Presently Santos reappeared, his thumbs hooked in his gun belt, his sombrero pushed back.

"Now?" Emery said.

"Now."

The night hid them but Fargo never knew but when they might blunder onto a Comanchero. He went slowly, warily, the Colt molded to his palm. It took a while. They had to work their way around the cabins and lean-tos until they came to the rear of the house. Once, as they passed a cabin, the door opened and an older woman shuffled out, closed it and hobbled toward the fire. Fortunately she didn't look to either side or she would have spotted them.

"I should have knifed her for the hell of it," Emery whispered.

"Get ahold on yourself."

"Easy for you to say. That's not your brother they've made into a laughingstock."

"Is that all that bothers you? What about the hell he's been through?"

"Like you keep saying, he shouldn't have tried to cross the Staked Plain. He brought it on himself, the idiot."

"I thought you cared for him?"

"There is love and there is love," Emery said.

Fargo circled another cabin and crept past another lean-to. Ahead was the house. Poorly built, made mostly of planks stripped from wagons and a few logs, it would be out of place anywhere but here. Why Santos wanted a house and not a cabin was a mystery only Santos could answer.

Fargo glided toward the back. Emery tried to dart past him but he blocked his way. "Go slow, damn it."

"I am sick of you telling me what to do."

Fargo was getting sick of having to tell him. "Then use your damn head. We have to stay alive for their sake."

A stout post had been embedded in the earth, and a metal ring had been attached. From the ring ran a ten-foot length of chain secured to the collar around Adam Broxton's throat. Adam was on his elbows and knees, his forehead pressed to the ground, in the grip of despair; he was weeping.

This time when Emery went to move past Fargo, Fargo let him. Emery ran to his brother and knelt and placed a hand on his shoulder. "Adam? It's me, Emery."

Adam's head jerked up and he exclaimed in horror, "Oh God. Now I'm seeing things." His eyes had dark shadows under them; his cheeks were emaciated hollows.

"Keep your voice down, damn it. Do you want them to hear?"

"Not you," Adam said. "Anyone but you."

"Did you think I wouldn't?"

Their exchange made no sense to Fargo. "What the hell is going on? Let's free him and find his wife and get out of here."

Adam shifted on his knees, the chain clinking. "Who are you?"

"The man your father hired to find you."

"My father?" Adam Broxton uttered a strangled bleat. "My father has been dead for going on fifteen years."

Fargo wondered if the man was raving. "How can that be? If he's dead, who hired me?"

"Since Emery is with you, it must have been my stepfather. He's always had it in for me, and now he went and did this."

"Where is she?" Emery asked.

"Go to hell."

With a snarl, Emery wrapped his hands around Adam's neck and squeezed. "Tell me, damn you! Tell me or I'll throttle the life from your miserable hide."

Shock delayed Fargo's reaction. Rushing in, he seized Emery's wrists and tore him off. "What in hell has gotten into you?"

Emery didn't take his eyes off Adam. "Which cabin is she in? Or would you rather she spent the rest of her days here like you're going to do?"

"What?" Fargo said, his confusion climbing.

"I didn't come here for him," Emery said with a nod at Adam. "I came to save Evie. She's all that matters."

"Did you hear him?" Adam said to Fargo. "This is what I've had to put up with. And you brought him here to torment me more."

Fargo had listened to enough. "I don't know what this about and I don't care. I'm getting you and your wife out." He bent to examine the leather collar.

Suddenly Emery has his derringer in his hand. "Forget him. Help me find Evie."

"Are you loco?"

"No. I'm in love." Emery turned. "Come on. We've wasted too much time. We'll go from cabin to cabin until we find her."

"The Comancheros will see us."

From behind Fargo came a throaty chuckle. "We wouldn't want that, would we, gringo?"

Fargo whirled, and swore.

They were all there, a ring of Comancheros, dozens of men and women, most with leveled weapons, all with smiles and grins and smirks. Except Ria, who stood next to Santos. Wilson was at the leader's other elbow, a cocked Remington trained on Fargo.

"Say the word, boss, and I'll blow out his wick."

"And deprive us of what is to come? No, amigo. *Á caballo dado no se le mira el colmillo.*"

Fargo's Spanish was rusty, but he thought that Santos had just said not to look a gift horse in the mouth.

Emery still held his derringer. He pointed it at the Comanchero leader and shrilly rasped, "Where is she? Tell me or you are by God dead."

Santos's eyebrows arched. "Who is this madman, then? Or should I say mad boy?"

"I mean it." Emery took aim. "I came for her and I'm not leaving without her."

"This female you are so fond of, senor?" Santos calmly asked. "Who is she?"

"You know damn well. Evie. The woman I love."

Santos seemed as confused as Fargo. He nodded at Adam and said, "But she is his wife, no?"

"I'm his brother," Emery said, and amended it with "His stepbrother, actually. But she loves me. Not him."

"Ah. I think I see." Santos laughed. "But can this really be?"

Fargo made no move to use his Colt; he would be shot to ribbons. He stood stock-still and stared at Ria, who averted her eyes.

"Tell me more, senor," Santos was saying. "I would hear of this great love you and your brother's wife share."

"Take me to her, or else."

"Threats do you no good, young one."

"If you think I won't shoot, you are mistaken."

Santos sighed. "I weary of your bluster." He gestured at Wilson. "If you would be so kind, amigo."

The Remington cracked. Emery screeched and dropped the derringer and clutched at the stump of his index finger. Blood spurted and he cried, "No, no, no, no, no."

"Wilson," Santos said.

"My pleasure." The burly gun shark walked up to Emery, who was doubled over and mewing like a kitten, and almost casually slammed the butt of the revolver against Emery's head.

Emery wound up in a heap, unconscious.

"Like taking milk from a baby."

Santos turned to Fargo. "Now it is your turn, senor. Drop your *pistola, por favor.*"

Fargo let the Colt fall.

"*Bueno. Gracias.* You are smarter than the young one. A wolf, too, I think, where he is a sheep. What is your name?"

Fargo told him.

"You are being reasonable. I like that." Santos came closer. "Perhaps you wonder how we were able to catch you unawares."

Fargo gazed at Ria. "I can guess."

Ria finally looked at him. "I'm sorry. I told you. These are my people. I could not let them come to harm."

"And here you are," Santos said with a grin. "Like a fly into a spider's web."

The ring of gun muzzles gave Fargo gooseflesh. All it would take was a nervous twitch, and if one gun went off, they all might. "Any chance you can have them lower their hardware?"

"Certainly, senor. After you and the boy are tied. Later we will talk, you and I. Or are you like him, and you think you will not tell me what I want to know?"

"I'm not hankering to die," Fargo said.

"Excellent. You are reasonable. So am I, hombre. We will get along fine, you and I."

"What happens after?"

"After, senor?"

"After we've had our talk."

"Do you truly need to ask?"

9

The cabin was old and falling down. Part of the roof had collapsed and the bare earth floor was choked with weeds. It was in the woods past the freight wagons.

Fargo lay on his side. His wrists had been tied behind his back and Wilson had made him bend his legs back and the rope had been tied tight around his ankles. So tight, he couldn't move his arms or legs. So tight, his fingers were numb. So tight, he couldn't get at the Arkansas toothpick in his boot.

A lamp had been set nearby. Two other figures were bathed in its glow: Emery and Adam Broxton. Both were similarly trussed.

Just outside the open front door stood the Comanchero left to stand guard. He looked in at them from time to time and once came over to test their bonds.

Fargo was puzzled by why Santos had seen fit to include Adam. But then, a lot of what had happened in the past half an hour puzzled him. He was also disgusted with himself for being caught. He'd trusted Ria and she betrayed them. It wasn't the first time a beautiful face had made him do something he regretted, and if he lived through this it probably wouldn't be the last.

With an effort Fargo shifted toward the two stepbrothers. "One of you mind telling me what the hell that was all about out there?"

"No," Emery said.

"How about you, Adam?"

Adam had his back to them. He still wore the dog collar. His shoulders were moving, as if he were silently crying.

"Adam?"

So softly Fargo barely heard him, Adam said between sniffles, "There is no God. You know that, don't you? If there was, how could any of this have happened?"

"I want to hear about your stepbrother and your wife."

"You heard him."

"Explain it to me. I can be thick between the ears sometimes."

Adam sniffled, and shifted his legs, and after a lot of trying managed to roll over. His cheeks were wet with tears. "Don't you ever think about things like that?"

"Like what?"

"God."

"Did you get hit on the head when they caught you?"

"Maybe you're more like Emery, there. He never thinks about things like God and love and respect. All he thinks of is himself. He is all about him and what he wants. And what he wants, you see, what he has wanted for a very long time, is my wife."

Fargo glanced at Emery. "Anything to say?"

"Go to hell, the both of you."

Adam uttered a brittle laugh. "That's my stepbrother. He is so used to getting his way that when he doesn't get it, he turns mean. He's killed, you know."

"I know," Fargo said. "About your wife?"

Adam was a while responding. More tears flowed, and then he coughed and said quietly, "She's the finest person I've ever met. Sweet and gentle and loving. The happiest day of my life was when I asked her to be my bride and she accepted. But that's what set Emery off."

"Set him off how?"

"He had always been nice to Evie. More nice than I ever saw him be to anyone. When I brought her around he would talk to her and fetch tea for her and was the perfect gentleman. Little did I know he secretly lusted after her. He wanted her for his own."

Emery raised his head. "She'll be mine yet. You wait. It was a mistake for her to marry a weakling like you. She must realize that by now."

"You see?" Adam said to Fargo, and went on. "After I announced that I was marrying her, he became vicious. He badgered her to marry him, instead, and was always trying to goad me into a fight. I refused."

"Coward," Emery said.

"He's the reason we left. I wanted to be as far from him as I could get. We were thinking about going on to California, but now . . ." Adam stopped and did more sniffling.

"Yellow cur coward."

"What did Abe say about all this?" Fargo asked.

"My wonderful stepfather? He said he was neutral but he was partial to Emery. He's always been partial to his own boys and treated me as if I were an outsider. As if I had no right to live in the house I grew up in." Adam paused. "But then, he's a miserable bastard who married my mother for her money."

Emery raised his head again. "Don't talk about my pa that way. I won't stand for it. He's always treated me decent."

"He's always spoiled you is more like it," Adam replied. "He gives you anything you want. And now he's tricked this man into bringing you to me so you can try and take Evie again."

"We didn't trick him, exactly," Emery said with a sly grin. "We just didn't tell him the whole truth."

Fargo made himself another promise then and there.

"I bet you didn't count on anything like this?" Adam said to his stepbrother. "You outsmarted yourself this time. You came to take my life and steal my wife, but now you're going to lose yours. Fitting, I would say."

"I'm not dead yet."

From the doorway Ria said, "You will be soon enough. Santos is coming for you when the sun is up."

Fargo hadn't heard her enter. The guard didn't try to stop her as she came over and knelt next to him. She was as lovely as ever, and the scent of her, so close, was intoxicating. He craved her as a starving man craved food or a man dying of thirst in the desert craved water.

"I'm sorry," Ria whispered.

"A little late," Fargo said.

"I regret what I have done. It seemed the right thing to do but now I am sad."

"Cut me loose."

Ria touched his cheek. "I can't. I do not have a knife. All I can offer is an apology."

"A hell of a lot of good that does me."

"They are my people."

"So you keep saying." Fargo supposed he shouldn't be so hard on her but how could he not be when thanks to her he had mere hours to live? "Tell it to yourself again after Santos slits my throat. Maybe it will help you sleep better."

"He will not kill you so quickly, I am afraid. He will do many terrible things to you and these others first."

Adam stopped sniffling to say, "You don't mean me, too? Haven't I always done as he wants? Don't I act just like a dog for him? He's said that he is fond of me."

Fargo's disgust knew no bounds.

"Santos has tired of you," Ria informed Adam. "He tires of all his pets eventually. He thinks it fitting you die with your brother."

Adam turned to Emery. "Do you see what you've done? You and your damn selfishness have gotten me killed. I hate you. I hate you more than anything. I wish to God my mother never met your father."

"Infant," Emery said.

"Do you see?" Adam said again, this time to Fargo. "Do you see what I had to put up with? Is it any wonder my wife and I wanted to leave Texas and start over somewhere else?"

"Don't bring Evie into this," Emery said. "She didn't want to leave. It was your notion."

"That's an outright lie."

They went on squabbling. Fargo shut them out. He was sick and tired of listening. Suddenly warm lips brushed his ear.

"I do not want you to die," Ria whispered.

"Makes two of us," Fargo replied.

"I will help you, but only you. These other two are for Santos to deal with. All I ask is your word that you will leave without harming anyone and never come back."

"You have it. Cut me loose."

"Not now," Ria whispered, her breath warm on his skin. "Later, after everyone else has turned in, I will come back."

"What about the guard?"

"Leave him to me." Ria straightened and smiled and said loud enough for the Comanchero outside to hear, "You only have yourself to blame. Adios, handsome one."

Fargo would like to believe her but she was the reason he was lying there like a lamb for the slaughter. He determined not to wait but to escape on his own. The problem was *how* when he could barely move. Using his elbows and his feet for leverage, he swiveled toward the bickering brothers. "Do you two idiots want to die?"

"What kind of question is that?" Emery snapped.

"No, of course not," Adam said sullenly.

"Then we have to work together," Fargo proposed. "One of you needs to untie my feet."

"Your feet?" Emery said. "What good will that do? We should untie your hands first."

"My feet," Fargo insisted. So he could slide his fingers into his boot and get hold of the toothpick.

"You make no kind of sense. But I'll see what I can do with part of a finger shot off."

Adam didn't offer to help. He lay there crying, and every now and again he whimpered.

With one eye on the guard, Fargo maneuvered so that his boots were near Emery's hands. Emery immediately set to work, prying hard at the knots. Whenever the guard so much as twitched, Fargo would whisper and Emery stopped. Once the Comanchero looked over his shoulder and then turned back.

Thank God for boredom, Fargo thought. Presently he felt the rope give a little. He tried to move his legs, but the loops weren't loose enough.

All the while, Adam cried.

"Have you ever met such a weak sister in your life?" Emery said. "What she saw in him I'll never know."

"Not now," Fargo said.

"I can't help it. I love her."

"She's married to your brother."

"*Step*brother," Emery stressed. He continued to pry and said between grunts, "We've never gotten along, him and me. From the day we met I thought he was next to worthless. He has no sand. No grit. No backbone."

"He tried to cross the Staked Plain in a Conestoga."

"That wasn't backbone. That was fear. He wanted to get away from me. He would have gone east instead of west but he figured west would be harder for me to find them."

The guard stretched and pushed his sombrero back on his head.

"I'd have stopped him, but he slipped away in the middle of the night. Outfitted the wagon without anyone knowing and then left a note saying where they were going."

The rope was looser. Fargo could move his legs apart about an inch. He sought to work his fingers into his boot but couldn't quite manage.

"Do you know what he was afraid of? That she'd leave him for me. That she'd prefer a man over a mouse."

Fargo wished Emery would shut up. He glanced at the door to be sure the Comanchero hadn't noticed what they were up to and his gut balled into a knot. The man was in the doorway, a hand on his revolver.

"What is it you do there, gringos?"

Emery stopped tugging and rolled partway onto his back. "We're talking, is all, Mex."

"Do not call me that, senor."

"You are one, aren't you? Mexican, I mean. Or are you a half-breed? I can never tell you mongrels apart."

The Comanchero drew his revolver. "Santos said he wants you alive, but he didn't forbid us to break bones."

"Figures," Emery spat. "You're not man enough to fight me fair."

"You are a fool, gringo. Fair is for the weak. I never use the word. Because for me the important thing is to live."

"Beat on me, then, you son of a bitch."

"I will," the Comanchero said. Gripping the revolver by the butt, he raised it over his head. "I will beat on you enough that you will learn to keep your mouth shut but not so hard that Santos will get mad at me." He came in. "I will enjoy this."

"Go to hell."

There was a loud thud as of a fist hitting a watermelon. But the Comanchero hadn't moved. His arm was still raised, his revolver poised. He took a staggering step as scarlet ribbons flowed from under his sombrero and down over his face and chin and neck. A single gasp escaped him. Pitching to his knees, he swayed, his arms drooping to the ground. "Who?" he said, and fell on his face in the dirt. His legs twitched a few times and he was still.

Chaku filled the doorway. In his huge hand was his war club, dripping fresh blood.

"About damn time," Emery said. "Where the hell have you been? You're supposed to watch over me."

"You told me to stay with horses."

"All right, all right. Cut me loose."

Chaku came to Fargo and knelt. "I free you first."

"What the hell?" Emery said.

That was when a large black dog poked its head in the door and snarled.

10

The Katonza was incredibly quick. He whirled and was on the dog before it could bark. His club was a blur. There was another thud and a crunch and the dog was flat on its belly with its legs splayed from the force of the blow and its tongue jutting limp over its lower jaw.

"Damn," Fargo said in admiration.

Chaku drew his knife and cut Fargo free. He did the same for Emery, who stiffly rose and groused, "You should have done me first. You're my pa's slave, not the scout's."

Fargo rubbed his wrists and hands to restore circulation. "I'm obliged."

The Katonza cut Adam's ropes but Adam didn't move. His eyes stayed shut, his cheeks moist from all his crying.

"Adam?" Fargo said.

Adam didn't respond.

"Adam?"

"What?"

"You're free. Get up. We're going to find your wife and escape."

"No."

"You'd rather stay here and be killed?"

"I know what's going to happen now. I'd rather die. Go without me. Take her and good riddance."

Disgust filled Fargo. *This* was the man he had come so far at such great risk to save? He went over and poked Adam's shoulder with the toe of his boot. "Get up, damn you."

"No. I tried and I failed. I can't live without her, so it will be a blessing, really."

"What the hell are you talking about?"

Emery said with ripe scorn, "He's talking about me."

"Damned lunkheads." Bending, Fargo slid his hands under Adam's arms and brought him to his feet. Adam was so thin it was like lifting a feather.

"Don't. Please."

Fargo's disgust was changing to anger. "Listen to me, Broxton—"

"Yoder," Adam said.

"What?"

"My name is Adam Yoder. My mother remarried, remember? My father was Frank Yoder, her first husband."

"All right, Yoder. If you want to give up, fine. But you'll do it *after* I get you and your wife out."

"What difference does it make when?"

Fargo grabbed him by the tatters of his shirt. "You owe it to me for all I've had to go through to find you."

"That's ridiculous."

Fargo came close to punching him. It took every ounce of will he possessed not to. Instead, he shoved Adam toward the door, saying, "You're coming whether you want to or not. Lag and you'll wish you hadn't."

"You're just like my stepbrother," Adam said. "You don't care about the feelings of others."

"And you're about the biggest jackass I've ever met." Fargo looked out. The valley lay quiet under a plentitude of stars. The cabins and lean-tos were dark. He saw no other dogs and hoped most of the Comancheros took their pets inside at night. "Which cabin is Wilson's?"

Adam just stood there.

"I won't ask you twice," Fargo said.

As slow as molasses, Adam raised an arm and pointed at

a cabin across the way. "There. That's his. That's where Evie is. Go get her and leave me be."

"I can knock you out and throw you over my shoulder."

"I hate the world," Adam said sorrowfully.

Fargo had never met anyone quite like this baby in a man's body. He gripped Adam's wrist and pulled. "Come on, you worthless bastard."

The night dappled them in welcome shadow. A wind out of the northwest rustled the oaks and willows. Frogs croaked and crickets chirped and way off in the outside world a coyote yipped, its cry faint and eerie.

Fargo put his hand on his empty holster and scowled. He would dearly love to have his Colt. He imagined that one of the Comancheros wound up with it.

Adam dug in his heels and said much too loudly, "I don't want to go any farther."

It was the last straw. Fargo hit him. Flush on the jaw and hard enough that Adam buckled and would have fallen except that Fargo got a shoulder under him and hoisted him up.

Fargo scanned the cabins. No one came out to investigate. No light appeared in any of the windows. He moved faster, his burden no burden at all.

Emery chuckled. "I wish that had been me done that. I've wanted to hit him for so long."

"Shut the hell up." Fargo was fed up with both of them. The Broxtons had lied to him, used him to Emery's ends. When he claimed the other half of the money due, he just might do to Abe Broxton as he had just done to Adam.

They neared Wilson's cabin. Fargo slowed and motioned at Chaku and then at Adam. The Katonza nodded and easily lifted Adam onto his own broad shoulder.

Emery went to go on by them but Fargo stepped in front of him and shook his head.

On cat's feet, Fargo moved to the door and put an ear to

the wood. From within came sounds. A rhythmic creaking, and then a woman's voice, saying, "Oh! Oh! Like that. Yes, like that."

Fargo turned to Emery. "Stay put." To Chaku he said, "If he tries to follow me, knock him over the head with that club of yours."

"You better not," Emery said.

Fargo tried the wooden latch. It moved with the slightest of scrapes. He inched the door open enough to stick his head in. The inside was black as pitch but he could make out a doorway on the right. A bedroom, he reckoned. He closed the door behind him and crept toward it.

The woman giggled. "You're so deliciously wicked. No one has ever done the things to me that you do."

"Move your ass, not your mouth," Wilson said.

Fargo nearly collided with a table. Just in time he stopped and went around, his fingers sliding over the top. They brushed something hard, something metallic. He groped, thinking it might be a knife. It was a revolver. More specifically, it was *his* revolver. He had used the Colt for so long, held it so many countless times, that he could tell by the feel of the grips and the balance.

Chance had favored him. Fargo grinned and checked that it was loaded by touching the holes in the cylinder to be sure each held a cartridge.

The creaking resumed.

Fargo stalked to the bedroom doorway. By now his eyes had adjusted enough that he could make out two figures on a small bed. The man was on his back, the woman on top, riding him. Wilson began to grunt. The woman was panting.

"Yes. Yes. I'm almost there," she husked. "Oh God. You're an animal and I love it."

"Shut up, bitch."

Fargo edged into the room and along the wall, placing each

boot lightly. He came up behind the woman, her body blocking him from Wilson.

Suddenly she threw back her head and groaned. "I'm coming! I'm coming!"

Wilson grunted louder than ever. The bed practically shook apart.

Fargo chose that moment. He took a bound and brought the Colt slashing down. Wilson's head was a dark circle. Fargo struck once, twice, three times.

The woman kept rising up and down. Either her eyes were closed or she was so caught up in bliss that she hadn't realized what Fargo had done. "Why did you stop? Keep going. Please. I want more. I always want more."

"Evie Yoder?" Fargo said.

She started. "Who's that? Who's there?"

"My name is Fargo. I've come to get you out of here."

"Wilson told me about you. You're the one came with Emery."

"That's right," Fargo said. He was impressed by how she perched so calmly on the man she had just made love to.

"They are like bad pennies," Evie said.

"Who?"

"Men." Evie slid off Wilson and lowered her feet over the bed. She stood up so close to Fargo that her breath fanned his face. In the dark he could not tell much other than that she had ample breasts and hair that hung past her shoulders.

"Throw some clothes on."

"Why?"

"I just told you. I'm getting you out."

"What's your hurry? You and me could have some fun." Evie put her hand on his chest. "A quick one before we go."

"Are you loco?" Fargo was asking that a lot lately.

"You don't like women?"

The pressure of her hand and the warmth of her body made

Fargo's skin prickle as if from a heat rash. "I like women fine. But your husband and Emery and Chaku are waiting outside."

"Oh God. Adam is with you? Then go by yourselves. I don't want to hear him."

Fargo was losing his patience. "Lady, I've gone to a lot of trouble to save your skin."

"Did it ever occur to you I might not want to be saved?"

Fargo swore. The whole damn family was as crazy as loons. "You're being held captive by Comancheros."

"Not anymore. I'm Wilson's woman. I get to do pretty much as I want." Evie chuckled. "He was easy to win over. Most men are once they've had me."

Fargo took a step back. "Put clothes on or I'll take you as you are."

"Wouldn't that be something? Me, prancing around in the altogether. It would give Adam and Emery a thrill."

"We don't have all night."

Evie bent down. "My dress should be here somewhere." She turned from side to side. "Ah. Here it is. Give me a second."

Fargo heard rustling and then she was beside him, her arm brushing his.

"Ready?"

"I can't wait to see you in the light. You have a nice voice. Do you have a nice face to go with it?"

"Honest to God," Fargo said in exasperation.

"What?"

Fargo was anxious to be shed of the Comanchero haven. He led her out and no sooner were they over the threshold than Emery squealed in delight and went to embrace Evie but she pushed him back.

"No, you don't."

"What's the matter with you? It's me."

"I have eyes," Evie said.

She had a lot more, Fargo saw. She had beautiful green eyes set in a gorgeous face. She had natural ruby red lips.

She had golden hair that shimmered in the starlight like spun silk. A green dress clung to her hourglass body.

"Chaku," Evie said to the Katonza.

"Miss Yoder."

"Still fond of Rohesia?"

"Yes, Miss Yoder."

"Too bad. It isn't often a man passes up a chance with me. I wouldn't have told her, you know."

Emery said, "Stop talking like that. You know you never would. Not with him. It's me you love. You told me that night in the stable."

"I say a lot of things."

Fargo had it then. He saw it all, and he almost laughed. But a loud snore from the open window of another cabin brought him back to the here and now. "Enough!" he whispered. "We're getting the hell out of here while we can. Follow me, and no talking."

Dozens of horses were in a rickety corral. Other animals were in a long string over near the trees.

Fargo hurried to the corral. The gate consisted of two thick poles. He lowered them and moved among the horses. Quiet coaxing and smacks on the rump induced them to file out. Some went off up the canyon. The rest milled, uncertain what to do.

Fargo made for the string. A bay nickered and stamped as he went down the line untying each animal. When he was done he waved his arms and smacked a few and they merged with the horses near the corral. He held on to the reins to two of them. Emery and Chaku helped him drive the rest up the canyon. They went slowly so as not to create a racket that would rouse the Comancheros.

Evie acted amused by it all. "This won't help you much. A lot of these horses will drift back."

"Every minute helps," Fargo said. He was glad when they were well out of earshot of the cabins.

Emery fell into step with Evie. "We need to talk."

"Not now."

"I need to know. Did Wilson touch you? Did he force himself on you? Tell me true."

Smiling radiantly, Evie Yoder said, "He never laid a finger on me."

"Thank God. I was worried sick. A sweet angel like you in the hands of a brute like him."

There were moments in Fargo's life, and this was one, when the absurdity of it all had him hankering for a bottle of good whiskey. He liked that word, absurdity. He heard a parson use it once and he had asked what it meant and the parson said it meant too ridiculous to be believed.

The next moment Fargo's reverie was shattered by wild shouts from back up the canyon.

The Comancheros had discovered they were gone.

11

They broke into a run.

Fargo took the lead, pulling the two horses after him. Chaku effortlessly kept pace, Adam's unconscious form swinging like a pendulum. Emery stayed at Evie's elbow.

Fargo hoped the Comancheros would waste time searching for their missing mounts. Every minute helped.

"You keep bumping me," Evie said to Emery.

"Not on purpose, dear one."

"Don't call me that. And I don't like you so close. I thought I made it plain how I feel."

"You made it plain that I am the man for you. Not in so many words. But in the way you were with me."

"When will I learn?" Evie said.

That they could squabble while fleeing for the lives was a wonderment. "Hush up," Fargo told them. "I need to hear if we're being chased."

The Ovaro and the other horses were where they had been left. Fargo motioned at the pair he had brought and said to Evie, "Climb on and we'll light a shuck."

"They don't have saddles."

"There wasn't time to saddle them." Fargo cupped his hands and held them ready to boost her.

"You expect me to ride bareback?"

"Unless you'd rather go on foot all the way back to Dallas."

"I've never ridden bareback in my life. In fact, I haven't done much riding at all."

"Practice makes perfect," Fargo said.

"Are you trying to be comical? If we go any faster than a walk, I'll fall off and break something."

"You're stalling," Fargo suspected. "Get the hell on or I'll throw you on and tie you down."

Evie smiled. "I love a forceful man."

"She can ride double with me," Emery said. He had already mounted. "Grab hold."

"I'd rather be shot than ride double with you. It would only encourage you in your folly."

Emery laughed. "You're only saying that to tease me."

Fargo was about to lose his temper—again. "You can ride with me," he said to Evie.

"Lucky me."

"Evie," Emery said.

"Don't start."

Chaku had thrown Adam belly-down over one of the horses and was climbing onto his own mount. "They come," he said.

Fargo heard them, too: the drum of boots from out of the canyon. He gripped the saddle horn and swung onto the Ovaro. "Take hold," he said to Evie

"Whatever you say, handsome."

They headed east, Fargo leading the pack animal, Chaku leading the horse that bore Adam, Emery wearing a scowl.

Evie pressed against Fargo's back and wrapped her arms around his waist. "My. Isn't this cozy?"

"We're running for our lives," Fargo mentioned.

"It's still cozy." Evie giggled and placed a hand on his thigh. "Let me know if I distract you."

"Damn, woman."

For a quarter of an hour they rode hard. Adam flopped like a limp rag. Fargo saw that he was about to fall off and called a halt. He dismounted, saying to Evie, "Stay on. This will only take a minute."

"Darn. I was hoping you and me could get better acquainted."

Emery was a boiling pot about to blow its lid.

Ignoring him, Fargo lowered Adam and slapped his cheeks. "Come on. Wake up."

Adam's eyelids fluttered.

Fargo slapped him again. "Wake up or I'll have to tie you down and you won't like that."

"What? Who?" Adam gazed about in confusion. He saw Evie and Emery, and groaned. "Oh. Now I remember."

Fargo nodded at the bareback sorrel. "That's yours to ride. The Comancheros are after us and I'm not anxious to tangle with them again."

"Where's my wagon?"

"Back in the canyon."

"You *left* it?"

"Be sensible," Fargo said. "There wasn't time to hitch a team." And even if there had been, a Conestoga couldn't outrun men on horseback.

"All my worldly possessions are on it," Adam protested. "Everything I own that those awful Comancheros didn't help themselves to."

"You still have your life."

"I'd rather have my wagon."

Fargo pushed him toward the sorrel. "Climb the hell on."

"Very well," Adam said sullenly. He gripped the mane. "But I want you to know I resent your behavior."

"I'm not fond of idiots so we're even."

"You are a terrible man," Adam said, but he climbed on, with difficulty, and awkwardly straddled the horse.

"We should have just left him," Emery said.

Fargo was sick of both of them. The only one he respected was the Katonza. He swung back on the Ovaro. "Stay in single file and don't lose sight of the person in front of you." As a prudent afterthought he said, "Chaku, you come last in case anyone strays."

The night was a comforting shroud. The Comancheros couldn't track unless they used torches. Fargo shifted in the saddle often to look back but saw no sign of any.

Along about the fifth time, Evie grinned and said softly in his ear, "You're doing this on purpose, aren't you?"

"I need to check our back trail."

"Sure you do." Evie wriggled against him. "Why not admit it? The real reason is you like to feel my body on yours."

"You think that's all a man is interested in?"

"I *know* that's all men are interested in. I've known it since I was thirteen and my uncle took me out to his stable to show me a new pony he'd bought."

"I have other things on my mind right now."

"Don't get me wrong. I'm not complaining. I like it as much as men. More, maybe. It's brought me no end of trouble, not being able to say no."

"You said yes to Wilson."

"I had to or he'd have hurt me. Truth was, he bored me. I had to talk as if he was the best lover ever but he was about as exciting as a tree stump. Some men have little imagination and he had none at all."

"No twinges of conscience?"

"What for? I'm not one of those women who think spreading her legs is a sin. I do what I do because I like to do it."

Fargo had to ask. "Why in hell did you get hitched?"

"We all make mistakes. Adam was like a puppy, so innocent and sweet. I couldn't say no. But I wasn't married a week when Emery took an interest and I couldn't say no to him, either."

"Or anyone else."

Evie laughed. "You have me figured out. So when is it your turn? No strings attached, I promise."

Fargo began to like her. She had a refreshing openness

about her needs. "Talk a little louder so Adam and Emery hear."

"God, I hope not. Adam will whine and Emery will demand and I'll be caught in the middle."

"You brought this on yourself."

"Yes," Evie admitted. "I should have put my foot down when Adam came up with his brainstorm about Arizona. He did it for me. He was afraid he'd lose me to Emery."

"So he ran. In a Conestoga."

"Isn't life silly?"

"Too damn silly for words," Fargo agreed.

They rode for a while without saying anything. Occasionally coyotes yipped and once the screech of a cougar pricked the Ovaro's ears.

Evie's cheek was on Fargo's shoulder, her breasts cushioned by his back. Gradually her hands slid lower and at length Fargo felt compelled to say, "Behave yourself."

She tittered in his ear. "Why, kind sir, whatever do you mean?"

"There is a time and a place," Fargo said. "This isn't it."

"Are you sure you like women?"

"I like them fine."

"Then any time or any place is good enough." Evie playfully nipped his earlobe. "Have you ever done it while riding a horse?"

"Charge the others to watch, why don't you?"

"I've done it on a horse. The bouncing makes it better. You don't have to do much but sit there."

"We're not making love."

"Is it that you're bashful? Or that you have religion? Or just that you haven't been with many women?"

"If you only knew."

"Then how about a poke when we stop? I'll slip away and you slip away and no one will catch on."

"Don't you ever get enough?"

85

"Never, ever."

Their banter was interrupted by a shout from Chaku. Fargo reined around, telling Adam and Emery to stop as he passed them. The Katonza had drawn rein and was gazing back the way they came.

"Do you hear?"

Fargo tilted his head. It was distant but unmistakable; riders were after them.

"How can they trail us in the dark?" Evie wondered.

"They're guessing," Fargo reckoned. "West, south and north would take us deeper into the Staked Plain. East is the shortest way to a settlement."

"We should hide and let them pass us," Evie suggested.

Fargo thought so, too. The only problem was that they were crossing a stretch of barren flatland with no cover.

"Why hide when can kill?" Chaku said.

Fargo debated. He'd like to whittle the odds. But a fight in the dark was a risky proposition. "For now we ride."

Adam kept lagging. It got so, Fargo fell back to ride alongside him.

"You're slowing us down."

"I'm sorry. My heart isn't in this."

"You'd rather be dead?"

"Yes."

Fargo swore under his breath. If he'd had any inkling of what he was in for when Abe Broxton hired him, he'd have told Abe to go to hell. "Emery would like that. It'll leave him free to fool around with your missus."

"She doesn't want him. She wants me." Adam smiled at Evie. "Isn't that right, dear heart?"

"God," Evie said.

"If you care for her that much, you should fight for her," Fargo said.

"I've done all I could," Adam replied. "I bought the Conestoga and was on my way to Arizona."

"That's your idea of fighting for her?"

"What else would you have me do? Shoot my own step-brother? Or take a knife to him maybe?"

"A punch on the jaw would be a good start."

"I'm not a violent person, Mr. Fargo. I never have been. I was teased for it a lot when I was younger but I can't help how I am."

"So you let everybody ride roughshod over you."

"You make it sound so terrible. But if everyone was more like me, this world would be a better place."

"The Apaches would like it. The Comanches and the Black-feet, too. Killing whites is their favorite pastime."

"You're being sarcastic. You're trying to make me mad so I'll care more. But what use is living when my own wife has given up on me?"

"You're the only one who can answer that. But if it was me, I'd punch Emery on the jaw."

In a swirl of dust Chaku was there. "They are close," he warned, pointing behind them.

Fargo listened. The rumble of hooves was a lot nearer. "We'll make a stand here." Rather that than a running fight with the Comancheros shooting at their backs.

"Don't expect me to fight," Adam said.

Fargo swung down and yanked the Henry from the scabbard. "Get off and get behind your horses."

Emery said, "Give me a gun. You'll need my help."

"If we do I will." Fargo jacked the lever to feed a cartridge into the chamber. He placed the Henry across his saddle and sighted down the barrel. It was like sighting into a well.

"They come quick" Chaku said.

Silhouettes appeared, men riding hell-bent for leather. At the same instant one of the Comancheros spotted them and bellowed, "There they are, boys! Get the bastards!"

12

Fargo centered the Henry on the foremost silhouette and fired. The Henry cracked and spat lead and the shape flung its arms wide and pitched to the earth.

The other Comancheros never slowed.

Fireflies flashed, attended by the boom of thunder. The packhorse whinnied and went down.

Fargo realized the Ovaro might be hit. He vaulted up and reined toward their attackers. A jab of his spurs, and he galloped to meet them headlong. The first was on him almost before he could blink. One-handed, he swung the Henry like a club and clipped the rider on the jaw. The man tumbled. Suddenly he was in a ring of Comancheros. He threw the Henry at one as the man sought to take aim. The Colt filled his hand, and he shot at a bearded face and then at a Comanchero wearing a sombrero. He thumbed the hammer and fired and thumbed the hammer and fired and then he was alone in a ring of riderless horses.

The man he had struck with the Henry was back on his feet and holding a revolver. "I've got you, you son of a bitch."

From out of the dark loomed Chaku. The Katonza's heavy war club described an arc and the top of the Comanchero's head caved in with an audible *crunch*, hat and all.

"I'm obliged," Fargo said.

The rest of the Comancheros were dead. Amazingly, the only casualty on their side was the packhorse.

"We're safe now, right?" Adam asked. "They won't send any more after us now that we've killed these."

"You helped, did you?" Fargo responded.

Evie said in annoyance, "Don't be a bigger fool than usual, Adam. Santos won't rest until he catches us. Every last Comanchero in their band is after us by now. These were just the ones who caught their horses first. We won't be safe until the Staked Plain country is well behind us."

"She's right," Emery remarked. "She's always right."

"Oh, please," Evie said.

Their bickering was fraying at Fargo's nerves. "Pick weapons. A revolver and a rifle for each of you."

Emery moved to the bodies.

"I'm not much of a shot," Evie said, "but I'll help best I can."

Adam stood there.

"What are you waiting for?" Fargo demanded. "A dead Comanchero to get up and give his revolver to you?"

"I don't feel right around dead people."

Emery snorted in derision. "No wonder Evie likes me more. You are next to worthless."

"Please don't," Evie said.

Chaku motioned at the three of them and said to Fargo, "I hit with club, our ears have rest, eh?"

Fargo laughed.

"I don't think that was funny," Emery said. "Wait until I tell Pa. He won't think it was funny, either."

"Worthless is contagious," Fargo said, and stiffened when the faint sound of three shots wafted to them from the west. Almost immediately someone answered with three shots from the south. Then there were three more from the north.

"What was that all about?" Adam wondered.

"Signals," Fargo said. The Comancheros had split up to search for them. The group to the west had heard their clash and signaled to the groups to the south and the north. All three would converge and be after them. "We have to hurry or they'll catch us."

"I would just as soon they did," Adam said. He still hadn't moved. "I have nothing to live for."

Fargo strode over and slapped him. Adam tottered and raised a hand to his cheek in astonishment.

"What did you do that for?"

Fargo smacked him again.

Adam took a step back and wailed, "Stop it! Stop hitting me. What on earth has gotten into you?"

"What do you care? You don't want to live anymore," Fargo said, and smacked him a third time.

Adam nearly fell. His knees gave but he stayed on his feet, crying, "Enough! I won't stand for this, you hear? You have no right."

"Out here there are no rights," Fargo replied. "Only this." And he hit him again.

Adam cocked a fist. "Damn it. I've taken all the abuse I'm going to."

"Have you?" Fargo swung, and Adam blocked it. Fargo swung again, and grinned when Adam blocked that one, too. "That's better."

"What?"

"There's hope for you." Fargo picked up the Henry and stepped to the Ovaro. "Now get some damn weapons and get on your damn horse."

"You did that on purpose?"

"Oh, hell, Adam," Evie said. "Don't you know anything?"

"I'm confused," Adam said.

"Imagine that," Emery chimed in.

Chaku showed his teeth in a rare smile. "You sure you not want me use club?"

Fargo sighed. "God, I need a drink."

There was no sense in wearing the horses out when they would need to rely on them later, so they rode at a walk.

Fargo didn't delude himself. As surely as the sun rose with the dawn, the Comancheros would find them. The end would be swift. Emery and Adam and Evie having guns meant little. None were good shots, and there wasn't enough sand between them to fill a thimble. It would be him and Chaku, mostly, against dozens of men as hard as steel.

The night crawled. Fargo never knew but when the drum of hoofbeats would herald a bloodbath. An hour went by, and then two. He breathed a little easier. It might be the Comancheros wouldn't find them until after the sun was up.

Too bad for the Comancheros. In the daylight he could take a lot more with him.

Evie appeared at his side. She was on a claybank they had taken from the Comancheros. It had a fine Mexican saddle, the horn solid silver. "This is some horse. It has a nice gait."

"Some do," Fargo said.

"Will we stop to rest soon or not?"

"Not."

"It won't make a difference, will it? They'll catch us."

"They'll catch us," Fargo said.

"Then why are you doing this? Leave us and go on alone. You'd stand a better chance of getting away."

"I agreed to a job."

Evie nodded. "You're a man of your word. But is it worth dying over? It wouldn't be for me."

"It's my word."

"I admire that but I can't say as I think it's very smart. Dead is dead." Evie leaned toward him and spoke so only he would hear. "Since they'll catch us anyway, why not stop and have a poke?"

"You never give up."

"Not when it comes to pokes. They're all I live for. And

since you're about the handsomest man I've ever come across, it would be a shame for you to get killed without us doing it."

"No, thanks."

"What can it hurt? A quick one. Then you can die with a smile on your face and I won't need to scratch my itch for a while."

Fargo looked at her. "You are a marvel."

"Thank you."

By the position of the Big Dipper it was pushing two in the a.m. when Fargo called a halt. "We'll rest the horses," he announced.

"Thank goodness," Adam said. "My backside is sore. I much prefer a wagon seat to a saddle."

"You would," Emery taunted.

Fargo walked to the west and surveyed the starlit horizon. Nothing yet. It puzzled him. The Comancheros wouldn't give up. Not this side of the grave. He turned to go back and nearly collided with Evie.

"How about right here and now?"

"What would the prairie dogs think?" Fargo moved to go around but she clasped his wrist. "This isn't the time or the place."

"It could be," Evie said, and clasped his hand between both of hers. "How about we go for a walk?"

"What about *no* don't you savvy?"

Evie glanced over her shoulder, then brazenly molded her body to his. "Admit it. You wouldn't mind. I'm easy on the eyes. Everyone says so."

"Modest, too."

Evie boldly placed his hand on her thigh and wiggled seductively. "Adam is lying down and Emery is pouting. They won't miss us."

"You have poke on the brain."

"Are you sure?" Evie slid his hand up her dress to the junction of her thighs.

"Are you really sure?" She slid his hand higher and covered her left breast with his palm. "I bet that feels good."

"No," Fargo said. He sounded as if he had a cold.

Giggling, Evie ran his hand back down. "You know you want to. Every man does."

Fargo had to cough to say, "Damn, you don't listen."

Evie stroked with his hand between her legs, up and down, up and down. She stopped where the warmth was greatest. "I can tell you are hungry for it. Admit it."

Fargo glanced at the others. Chaku had squatted near the horses. Adam was on his back, a forearm over his eyes. Emery was staring to the east with his hands on his hips.

"We're wasting time." Evie tugged to take him deeper into the dark, and Fargo went with her. "I knew it," she crowed.

"I haven't said yes yet."

"You will."

A good twenty yards out, Evie stopped and whispered, "We'll have to do it quiet or Emery will have a fit and Adam will bawl. I hate it when he bawls."

Fargo was thinking of the guns Emery had. He turned so he was facing her husband and her lover.

Evie hiked her dress above her knees, grinned and hiked it above her waist. Underneath, she was naked. The starlight lent her skin a satiny sheen. "See anything you like, big man?"

"You asked for it," Fargo said. Cupping both of her mounds, he pinched her nipples, hard.

She gasped and squirmed and covered his hands with hers and pressed harder. "I like it rough."

"Good." Fargo bent, inhaled a nipple and bit it. Her nails raked his shoulders and her breath was hot in his ear.

"Yes! Like that."

Fargo plunged a hand between her legs. A flick of his finger, and her wet nether lips parted. He stroked her once, just once, and speared his finger up and in.

Evie rose onto the tips of her toes and her mouth parted

but she made no sound other than a sigh of contentment. He added a second finger and commenced to thrust.

"Ohhhhhh. I knew you would be good."

"Quiet," Fargo said gruffly. Below his belt his manhood had become a rigid pole. He pressed it against her legs and she looked down.

"Oh my. Is all of that you?"

The question was too stupid for Fargo to bother answering. He went on exciting her with his fingers as he reached down with his other hand to undo his belt buckle.

"Let me," Evie breathed. Eagerly, she pried and pulled and twisted and then his gun belt was around his ankles and his pants were around his knees and she cupped him, low down. "Goodness, you're big."

Fargo could scarcely breathe. He thought he would explode when she delicately traced a fingertip the length of his shaft.

"It's a shame we don't have much time," Evie whispered. "We make it out of this alive, how about the two of us lock ourselves in a hotel room and not come out for a week?"

"Glutton," Fargo said.

Taking a firm grip on his shoulders, Evie grinned. "This is a trick I learned when I was sixteen."

A swift motion, and Fargo's pole was enveloped in velvet wet and warmth.

Her mouth sought his and their tongues met. He cupped her bottom with his right hand and a breast with his left. She cooed and pumped up and down, slowly at first but with rising urgency.

Fargo matched her thrusts, their bodies grinding as one. He sucked on her tongue and licked her neck and bit an earlobe, inducing her to buck like a bronco out to throw its rider. Her body churned and heaved. She lifted her face to the stars and her eyes opened wide, and she gushed.

Fargo wasn't far behind. He rammed and rammed and then it was his turn. His whole body quivered and he exploded with the force of an erupting volcano. It went on and on until eventually he slowed and then stopped, drained and spent and content.

"That was grand," Evie said softly.

"I didn't think so," Emery Broxton said.

Fargo and Evie tried to turn but they were still hooked together and nearly fell.

"Damn," Fargo said. "When will I learn?"

"Your learning days are over." Emery tucked the stock of his rifle to his shoulder. "Any last words?"

13

Fargo would always wonder if Emery would have shot him; Emery never got the chance.

An ebony form reared and the rifle was wrenched from Emery's grasp. "I not let you kill him," Chaku said.

Emery grew livid. He bunched his fists and poised as if to spring but had the good sense not to. "How dare you? You're our *slave*. You don't tell *me* what to do. I tell *you*. Give me that rifle."

Chaku didn't answer—or give him the rifle.

"When I tell my pa—"

"Listen," Chaku said.

Fargo had been quickly putting himself together. He was strapping on the Colt and heard distant thunder that wasn't thunder. A bobbling pinpoint of yellow explained how.

"What's that?" Evie asked.

"They're tracking us by torchlight."

"They'll catch up sooner than we thought, won't they?"

"Appears so."

"Let them come," Emery growled. "I am in the mood to kill and it might as well be them."

They hurried to their horses. Fargo was set to mount when he saw that Adam was curled on the ground. Going over, he nudged him. "Time to fan the breeze."

Adam's eyes were closed and his hands were clasped between his legs. He looked for all the world like an infant in a crib. "Leave me be. I want to sleep."

"The Comancheros are coming."

"I don't care."

"They'll find you and kill you."

"I don't care."

Fargo resisted an impulse to kick him. Squatting, he shook Adam's shoulder. "You'll care if they torture you."

"Dying is dying."

"No, it's not. There is quick like a bullet to the brain or a blade to the heart. Then there is being staked out and skinned. Or having your tongue cut out and your ears chopped off. Or Santos might lop off your third leg. And that's just for starters. You'll suffer for hours or days. Is that what you want?"

Emery said with ripe scorn, "Let him lie there if he wants. The weakling deserves to die."

Fargo bent over Adam and said quietly, "What about Evie? With you gone, who will stand up for her?"

Adam opened his eyes.

"Why make it easier for your stepbrother?" Fargo whispered. "If it was me, I'd want to take a rock to his head."

"I've never killed. I don't know if I could."

"I didn't say to smash his skull to bits. A couple of good blows should discourage him."

"If only I could," Adam declared. "It would show Evie I'm not as puny as everyone thinks."

"It's something to think about." Fargo offered his hand. "What do you say?"

Adam sat up and took hold. "You're the only one who treats me halfway decent. Do you know that?"

Fargo didn't tell him the truth, that he was doing it to deprive Santos of the pleasure of torturing him, and to have an extra gun when the Comancheros caught up. "Just don't light into Emery until we don't need him anymore."

"When will that be?"

"When we've shaken the Comancheros." Fargo was being optimistic. Comancheros were human bloodhounds.

"Thank you."

On they rode at a trot. After half a mile Fargo slowed and looked back. He couldn't see the yellow light.

"They're still back there, aren't they?" Evie said.

"Yes."

A stretch of short-grass prairie brought them to broken country. Daybreak found them on the lip of a low rise, the first of a dozen or more bluffs that dotted the landscape like so many flat-topped mushrooms. Patches of brown rock and dirt showed amid the light green of grass and the darker green of mesquite and clumps of oak.

"I don't remember coming this way," Emery mentioned.

"We didn't. We're taking the shortest route out," Fargo informed him.

"Just so you don't get us lost."

"*Must* you always carp so?" Evie said. "He's doing his best to save us and all you do is gripe."

Emery shot her a withering look. "Listen to you. Are you his defender now? Was it that good with him?"

Evie didn't bat an eyelash. "Better than you by a long shot. Or I should say a long pole?"

"Mock me. But it made me see the truth. You don't love me. You never did. For you I was just another tumble in the hay."

"One of many tumbles," Evie said.

Emery turned to Adam. "I take back some of the things I said about you. I understand now. She's a whore and will always be a whore. Which still makes you stupid for marrying her."

Fargo reined in between them. "Save your spleen for when we shake the Comancheros."

"I won't forget you, either," Emery said.

Fargo gigged the Ovaro. A bluff ahead interested him. Partway up was a shelf littered with boulders. He hoped to find a way up to it but when he reached the bottom he found it too sheer to climb. He rode on just as dawn was breaking.

A golden arch blazed the eastern horizon. The stars were replaced by an ever-deepening blue as the sky rapidly brightened. A few cumulus clouds slowly drifted. Otherwise, it was clear.

Chaku came up next to the Ovaro. Dust caked the Katonza warrior and speckled his dark hair.

"You look for place to fight."

Fargo nodded. "We need to slow them. One man with a rifle could delay them long enough for the rest of you to get away."

"That man be you?"

"I'm the best shot."

"How many after us, you think?"

"Twenty. Thirty. Forty." Fargo shrugged. "I know what you're going to say. The odds are too great. I'm better off sticking with you."

Chaku grunted. "That not it. I say why fight twenty when only need fight one?"

"I'm listening."

"Kill their leader. Kill Santos. Maybe other Comancheros give up."

Fargo had thought of that. "He'll be the first one I shoot if I can."

"Have better chance if you have help."

Motioning at Evie, Adam and Emery, Fargo said, "Who would get those three out? One of us has to stay and it has to be you."

"I not like," Chaku said.

"You and me both." Fargo liked it even less that he was putting his hide at risk for people he didn't particularly care for.

Another bluff loomed. The top half was sheer, but a gradual slope rose to a mesquite-sprinkled knob forty feet up.

Fargo drew rein. He explained what he was about to do, and why. "I'll hold them as long as I can. Ride hard and by nightfall you should be far enough ahead they'll never catch you."

"What about you?" Evie asked.

"I'll follow as soon as I can."

Adam said, "You would sacrifice yourself for us? After how we've treated you?"

"I don't aim to die," Fargo assured him.

Emery uttered a bark. "Don't this beat all? Mister, you are as dumb as a clod of dirt. I wouldn't lift a finger for any of them now that it's sunk in how Evie is."

"Go to hell," Evie said.

"What will we do for food and water now that we don't have you to find them for us?" Adam asked.

"Chaku is good at living off the land," Fargo answered. "He'll get you out if anyone can."

"The darkie is from Africa," Emery said. "What does he know about Texas?"

"He can hunt game and find water and that's what counts." Fargo tapped his spurs to the Ovaro and headed up the knob. "Make yourselves scarce. There's no telling how soon they will show."

"Take care," Evie called up.

"Good-bye," Adam said.

Emery cackled. "Good riddance is more like it. If I ever set eyes on you again, it will be too soon."

The top wasn't flat. Near the edge was a trough worn by erosion that suited Fargo's purpose. He reined behind a boulder, slid down and shucked the Henry. Opening a saddlebag, he took out a box of ammunition. It was only half-full but it would have to do.

The trough was deep enough that when Fargo knelt, only his head showed. He took off his hat and placed it next to him, then curled his legs and braced his shoulder. He already had a round in the chamber, so he was set.

High in the sky a hawk soared on outstretched wings. Nearby, a blue grouse called. To the southwest was a prairie dog town. Prairie dogs scampered about until the hawk began to circle. Then one whistled and they vanished down their holes.

A kit fox appeared, meandering among the mesquite. A little later a pair of coyotes were briefly visible. To the northwest, dots grew into pronghorn antelope that drifted in his direction. Since the wind was blowing from them to him they didn't detect his scent. They were a quarter mile out when they stopped and stared to the west and then bolted.

It wasn't long before Fargo spied what their sharper eyes had seen: an approaching dust cloud. He cradled the Henry and marked the minutes as the cloud swelled and riders swept toward the bluff. At the forefront rode Santos and Wilson.

"I am plumb silly," Fargo said, and took aim.

Santos straightened and pointed at the spur. Fargo swore. Sunlight had gleamed off the brass receiver, giving him away. A careless mistake, worthy of a greenhorn. Fargo rushed his shot and knew even as his finger curled that he had missed.

Santos broke to the right, Wilson to the left. The Comancheros behind them followed suit. It was as if a giant meat cleaver had split them down the middle.

Fargo snapped a shot at Santos and then at Wilson. The former was unscathed. The latter swayed slightly. Fargo levered in another round to finish Wilson off—only to have the second-in-command disappear into a wash or gully.

It wasn't going well. Fargo lined up his sights with another rider and fired and the man toppled. He aimed and repeated the performance.

Fargo unleashed a leaden hailstorm. He pumped the lever, fired, jacked the lever again. That two more went down was small consolation. There were too damn many.

The rest gained cover.

Fargo fed a cartridge in. Without warning, rifle barrels bristled like quills on a porcupine. He threw himself flat. Above him lead buzzed and zinged and kicked up showers of dirt.

Fargo stayed low until the firing stopped. Warily sitting up, he peered over.

No one showed themselves. He set to replacing the cartridges he had used.

A black sombrero and then a bearded face rose out of the wash; it was Santos. Fargo jerked the Henry to his shoulder but Santos held up his hands to show they were empty and smiled.

"Is that you up there, gringo? The scout?"

Fargo saw no reason not to say, "One and the same."

"Show yourself. I give you my word we will not shoot."

Fargo laughed.

"Very well. You do not trust me." Santos rose a little higher. "Where are our captives, gringo? Where is Dog and Wilson's *puta*?"

"They must be in Dallas by now."

Now it was the Comanchero leader's turn to chortle. "I like you, scout. So I say this. Let us ride past without shooting at us and you can live. I only want those you took from us."

"That's generous of you."

"Practical. You have already killed some of my men. What do you say?"

"I say you don't want to take the long way around the bluff, and you think I'm stupid."

Santos said something to someone in the wash, then looked up. "Why die for them? The best you can do is slow us some."

"That's enough," Fargo shouted.

"Do you know what, gringo? You have made me mad. That is not smart to do. Now I hope we take you alive. I will do things to you that—"

Fargo fired. At the blast, Santo's sombrero whipped back and Santos dropped. A minute dragged by with no reaction from the Comancheros, prompting Fargo to holler, "Did I kill the son of a bitch?"

"No, gringo, you did not," Santos yelled back. "And now it is our turn."

He bellowed, and the Comancheros swarmed out of the wash and from other points of concealment.

"Hell," Fargo said.

14

The Henry was a remarkable weapon. Fargo used to rely on a Sharps but had switched. Not because the Henry was more powerful; it wasn't. When it came to knocking down a buffalo or a bull elk, his old Sharps had the Henry beat. But the Sharps was a single-shot rifle. A man could load a Henry on Sunday, as the saying went, and shoot it all week. An exaggeration, but the Henry did hold fifteen rounds in a tubular magazine under the barrel. Insert a cartridge into the chamber before loading, and a man had sixteen ready to use.

Fargo had reloaded while Santos was talking and now he cut loose. He fired, worked the lever, fired again. He fired as fast as was humanly possible and made each shot tell.

Eight Comancheros were down, dead or wounded, when the charging tide reached the bottom of the knoll. Fargo's withering fire broke them as rocks break an incoming wave. They wavered, and another fell, the last man screaming as he went down. That did it. They retreated, some shooting as they went, seeking whatever cover was handy.

Fargo stopped firing. He didn't have enough lead to waste any. Quickly, he reloaded, then patted the Henry and smiled. It had been a big decision, giving up the Sharps. Moments like this justified it.

Oaths rose from the wash. In Spanish, Santos lavished insults on Fargo, on Fargo's mother.

Fargo let him rage. When Santos fell silent, he added insult by laughing and calling down, "Is that the best you can do?"

Santos indulged in more oaths.

Several of the wounded Comancheros were trying to crawl back. Others were too badly hurt to do more than cry for help.

"Get your people," Fargo shouted.

"What was that, gringo?"

"You heard me. I won't shoot."

"You expect us to trust you?"

"It's either that or watch them bleed to death."

An argument ensued in the wash. Santos and Wilson, their voices raised. Then Santos said, "Very well, gringo. We will do as you say. Remember your promise."

"A truce until it's done."

"Very noble of you," Santos shouted.

Fargo smiled. Noble had nothing to do with it. When they came out of hiding, he could count how many were left. Besides that, the cries of the wounded might mask the sounds of other Comancheros trying to sneak up on him.

Santos did more bellowing. Reluctantly, half a dozen men appeared and hastily carried their fallen companions away. Some glanced at the knoll in dread of being shot. When the last of the wounded had been carted off, silence fell.

Fargo was content to sit and wait. The longer he held them, the better the odds of Chaku and the others getting away. He imagined the Comancheros were plotting how to slay him. A direct assault hadn't worked so they would try something else. Something devious.

"Gringo? Are you still up there?"

"I'm admiring the view," Fargo shouted back.

"If I stand up do I have your word you won't shoot?"

"You have it. But don't expect me to do the same."

The Comanchero leader did a brave thing; he rose and held his hands out as he had done the last time. His sombrero was pushed back, and he was grinning. "You are an hombre after my own heart, amigo."

"Is that a fact?"

"*Sí*. You will not believe me but I respect fierce men, and you are *muy* fierce."

"It's not fierce so much. It's grumpy. I'm always in a bad mood when I don't get my coffee in the morning."

Santos chuckled. "You crack jokes even now. You would make a good Comanchero, I think."

"No," Fargo answered honestly.

"Why not?"

"I have something you don't."

"What would that be?"

"A conscience."

Santos didn't take offense. "I had one once. It died when I was twelve, in Mexico. We were poor, and my *padre*, my father, he stole fruit to fill our empty bellies. Do you know what they did? They beat him and threw him in jail and at his trial the judge said they must make an example of him, so they hung him by the neck."

Fargo was interested despite himself. "For stealing fruit?"

"The orchard he stole from belonged to a man who was rich and powerful and a good friend of the judge."

"There are bastards everywhere."

Santos nodded. "Not long after that my mother became sick and was burning with fever. I went for help but no one would come near her and there was no doctor. I held her head in my lap and begged her not to die and the whole time she was praying to God to spare her. She died anyway." He stopped and gazed out across the Staked Plain. "That was the day I saw the truth. That was the day I learned there is no God."

"Go back," Fargo said.

Santos looked up at him. "What was that, gringo?"

"Take your people and return to your canyon. I won't shoot. I give you my word."

"Are you trying to be nice to us? I hope not. I would think less of you if you are."

"No more need die."

"Hell, gringo. We are all of us born to do just that."

Fargo tried another tactic. "Are they worth it, the woman and her husband? You can get another Dog. Wilson can find another woman."

"That is not the issue and you know it." Santos hooked his thumbs in his gun belt. "You took them from us and we cannot let that pass and call ourselves men."

"We always have a choice."

"Was my *padre* given a choice whether he would hang? Was my mother given a choice whether she would live? No and no. There is a lesson in their deaths. Do you not see?"

"I lost my parents, too."

"Then no more talk of choice. We are what we are and we do what we do and that is life."

Fargo sighed.

"I would like to have met you over a card game, gringo. We would be friends, I think."

"Take your wounded and go, damn it."

Santos bowed his head for a moment, and then flashed his devilish grin.

"I am sorry, senor. But for what it is worth, I will not let my people cut you up when you are dead. They do that sometimes when they have had friends shot and are mad. For you, though, I will show respect."

Fargo didn't say anything.

"Our talk is about over. All the trouble you have gone to, and it will be for nothing. We will catch them."

In the back of Fargo's mind a warning blared, his inner voice saying, *He is talking to hear himself talk; he is talking to distract you*. Fargo whirled.

There were two of them, just coming over the top, burly breeds armed with revolvers and rifles, their chests crisscrossed by bandoliers. He fired into the face of the first and the other shot at him. His shoulder stung and he answered in kind and both were down, twitching and bleeding.

In the stillness that followed, Fargo's ears rang.

"Pedro? Lomley?" Santos hollered. "Is the gringo dead?"

"No, he's not!" Fargo shouted, and whipped the Henry to his shoulder. Even as the shot boomed, the Comanchero leader dropped from sight into the wash. Fargo dropped, too.

For several minutes all was still, until furtive movement warned Fargo they were up to something new.

"Gringo!" Santos shouted. "Hombre! You are proving as hard to kill as an Apache."

"I take that as a compliment," Fargo replied.

"They are fierce, too, the Apaches," Santos shouted. "More fierce than you and I."

Fargo scoured the base of the spur and the slope that led up to his position.

"You are proving to be more trouble than our captives are worth," Santos yelled. "I cannot afford to lose more men."

"Then be smart and leave."

"If only it were that easy. We both know I can't."

Fargo turned and crawled away from the edge. When he was behind the boulder that shielded the Ovaro, he rose and shoved the Henry in the scabbard. The saddle creaked under him as he stepped into the stirrups. Staying low, he rode to the far end and down the far side. Once at the bottom he used his spurs.

With any luck it would be a good long while before the Comancheros discovered he was gone.

Another mile, and Fargo halted. He climbed down and let the Ovaro graze while he sat on a rock and watched his back trail.

A red ant crawled over his boot. A small rattler slithered from under a boulder and lay sunning itself. A large bee buzzed about some wildflowers.

Fargo continued to wait. Sweat trickled from under his hat and down his brow. A bead got into his left eye and stung. He wiped his sleeve across his eye but it still stung.

A dust cloud appeared. It was smaller than the last time. There were fewer, and they weren't riding as fast.

Fargo stood and walked to the stallion. Climbing on, he rode around a hillock speckled with scrub brush. Out came the Henry. He was on one knee at the crest when the Comancheros thundered into sight. He did not see Santos, so he chose one at random and blasted the man from the saddle at a range of three hundred yards. Fine shooting for a Henry.

The rest scattered.

Fargo ran to the Ovaro. Forking leather, he continued east. This time he only went half a mile. He drew rein in a cluster of oaks. Tying the reins, he climbed to a fork. It was half an hour before the dust cloud reappeared. He raised the Henry and centered on a silhouette but he didn't shoot until the silhouette became a Comanchero and the Comanchero was close enough that he could see that the man had a mustache but no beard. Fargo fired.

Once again the Comancheros scattered.

Fargo was out of the tree and in the saddle before all of them found cover.

Once more he used his spurs and it was well he did. He was out the opposite side of the stand when a withering hailstorm clipped limbs and sent leaves and slivers flying.

By now, Fargo reckoned, Santos was fit to burst a blood vessel. He hoped the Comanchero leader would realize that the cost outweighed his thirst for revenge. Then again, where human nature was concerned, there was no predicting.

Fargo was in no hurry. It would be a while before they were after him.

He came to a gully and went down the near side and up the other. Ahead lay a rolling plain. Tall grass, rare for the Staked Plain, brushed the bottoms of his stirrups. He stopped twice to look back. The first time there was nothing but the second time the dust cloud testified to human stubbornness.

"Damn them, anyhow."

Fargo rode on. He went twenty yards. Thirty yards. Forty. He was thinking of Chaku and Evie and the lunkheads and not paying attention to the tall grass when it parted and a half-naked swarthy form sprang. Fargo stabbed his hand for his Colt but iron arms encircled him and a shoulder slammed into his gut and he was unhorsed.

Two more—fully clothed—pounced. One was a white man, the other from south of the border.

Fargo fought. He lost the Colt and couldn't reach the tooth-pick, so he resorted to his fists and his elbows and knees. He knocked one off and clubbed the other but the third had a pistol out and the barrel caught him solid. His hat went flying and the world swam, and when it cleared, he was on his side with his hands and ankles bound.

"We got you, gringo," the breed gloated, scarlet drops trickling from a split lower lip.

"Santos knew this would work," said the white Comanchero.

"He sent us to circle around on ahead of you," explained the third. "He counted on you to keep going east and he was right."

"He always is," said the breed.

Fargo was too sore and battered and mad at himself to acknowledge their genius.

"Cat got your tongue, gringo?" The breed delighted in rubbing it in.

"You should speak while you still can," said the white one.

"They are right, senor," remarked South of the Border. "Santos will cut out your tongue for the trouble you have caused him. And that is just to start. He will do other things . . ." He left his voice trail off.

"I trust he'll use a sharp knife," Fargo said.

The breed laughed. "You have a sense of humor. Good. You will need one."

"I never go anywhere without it."

"Jest while you can," South of the Border said. "I wouldn't want to be you for all the gold ever found."

The hell of it was, they weren't exaggerating. Fargo twisted his neck and stared to the west and felt his blood run cold.

In the distance rose the dust cloud.

15

The white Comanchero had a mean streak; he kicked Fargo in the ribs. It hurt like hell. Fargo gritted his teeth and didn't show the pain but he did snarl at the culprit, "Do you beat on helpless old ladies, too?"

Swearing, the white raised his boot over Fargo's face. "I'll kick your damn teeth in."

"I wouldn't, if I were you," the breed said.

"Why the hell not?"

"Santos wants this one for himself, remember?"

"*Sí*," agreed South of the Border. "And you know how he gets when one of us does something he doesn't like. Remember Mills, Keller? Santos had him tied to a pole and set him on fire."

"Don't forget Wilson," the breed said. "He wants to do things to this scout, too."

"I would not want Santos *and* Wilson mad at me," South of the Border said.

The white Comanchero scowled and lowered his boot. "Damn them. Always so high and mighty."

"It would not be wise to let them hear you say that, amigo," South of the Border advised.

Fargo had a temporary reprieve. The dust cloud was a ways off yet. It would be twenty minutes before the rest of the Comancheros showed up.

"I'll go get our horses," the breed offered, and walked off.

South of the Border squatted and grinned at Fargo. "All the trouble you went to, eh, gringo?"

Fargo didn't answer.

The white Comanchero had set to pacing back and forth in an excess of anger. "I still say I should stomp on him some. We've lost good men thanks to this son of a bitch."

"Cut me loose and you'll lose more," Fargo said.

South of the Border chuckled. "You never give up, do you? I respect that. It is a quality I myself have."

Keller stopped pacing. "Kiss him, why don't you, you damned greaser?"

"I do not like to be called that."

"I'll call you any damn thing I want, Lopez."

Fargo racked his head for a way to turn their mutual resentment to his advantage.

Keller resumed pacing. After a spell he glanced at the dust cloud and said, "I wish to hell they would get here." Then he turned in the direction the breed had gone and said, "Where the hell is Mariposa? He should be back with the horses by now."

"You have no patience," Lopez said.

"I have enough."

Fargo rested his cheek on the ground. He was staring at the grass behind Lopez and saw the grass silently part and an ebony face appear. Chaku smiled at him, and the grass closed.

Keller took off his hat and wiped at his brow and put his hat back on. "If it were any hotter we would melt."

"Complain," Lopez said. "That is all you know how to do."

"Keep it up." Keller turned to the south again. "I don't care what you say. Mariposa is taking too long."

Lopez scratched his beard. "Perhaps you are right. One of us should go have a look."

"I'll go."

Keller took a single step and Chaku reared in front of him. Keller's hand flashed to his six-shooter but as quick as he was, the warrior was quicker. Chaku's war club caught Keller in the face and reduced his nose and cheeks to so much pulp. Bits of teeth and drops of blood splattered the grass as Keller tottered and fell.

Lopez was rooted in shock then grabbed for his revolver and had it halfway out when he stiffened and arched his back and reached behind him. His eyes grew wide and he moved his mouth but the only sound he made was a low groan. Keeling to his knees, he toppled over, dead. From his back jutted the hilt of a knife.

The grass rustled and out rose Emery. "I bet you're surprised to see us," he said as he wrenched the knife out.

"Cut me loose."

Hunkering, Emery wagged the bloody blade. "We came back to help. Good thing we did."

Fargo couldn't believe what he was hearing. He had gone through so much just so they would be safe. "You were supposed to be long gone by now."

"Blame her," Emery said, and jabbed his thumb over his shoulder.

Out of the high grass came Evie, smiling grandly, as if she had done the greatest thing in the world. "We saved you. We honest to God saved you."

Fargo held it in until the ropes were gone and he stood and reclaimed the Colt. Then he faced them. "What the hell are you doing here?"

"I told you," Emery said. "You have my sweetie to thank."

"That's right." Evie bobbed her chin. "I talked them into coming back. I was very persuasive."

Fargo looked at the Katonza and the warrior looked away. "There better be a good reason."

"There is."

Emery said, "I came because she promised to leave Adam and be with me if I did."

"Why would you do a thing like that?" Fargo asked her.

"For you," Evie said.

"For me why?"

"Just for you."

Fargo didn't savvy. She couldn't be saying she cared for him enough to risk her life. They hardly knew each other.

As if she sensed his confusion, Evie said, "If you need a better one, how about this? My intuition told me you needed us. So I talked Chaku and Emery into coming back. Emery was easy but Chaku took some doing. He kept saying as how you wouldn't like it."

"He was right."

"Is that any tone to take with someone you owe your life to?" Evie grinned and touched his chin. "Anytime you want to thank me proper, handsome, I'm agreeable."

"Here now," Emery said. "You gave your word it would be you and me and only you and me."

"Once we're man and wife," Evie said. "Which we won't be until we're back in Dallas."

Fargo was doing his best to catch up. "You're going to marry Emery? What happened to Adam?"

"He refused to help, so I told him I don't want anything to do with him anymore. Not that I did anyway."

"Where did he get to?"

It was Chaku who pointed.

Adam was bringing the horses. His head was down and his shoulders were slumped, his posture that of a condemned man walking to the gallows.

"Look at him," Emery said. "He doesn't deserve a fine gal like her. He gave her up as easy as I shed my socks."

"You are supposed to be miles from here," Fargo stressed.

Evie laughed. "You're upset that we saved you? How is that for gratitude? Or does it gall you that you're not the only one who can be valiant?"

Fargo didn't know what in hell she was talking about, and said so.

"You delayed the Comancheros so we could get away. If that's not valiant I don't know what is."

"It's not about valiant. It's about money. I'm being paid to take you back."

Fargo went to the Ovaro and snagged the reins. He was grateful but he was also concerned. The dust cloud was a lot closer. "By coming back for me you've put your lives in danger."

"I like good fight," Chaku said.

"I go where Evie goes," Emery declared.

Adam had arrived and heard them. "You can have her. After all I did to save our marriage, she betrayed me. I wish I had known what she was like when I married her. I never would have said 'I do.'"

"Don't be so dramatic," Evie scolded.

"I did as you asked and brought the horses. Now I want to be on my own." Adam climbed on his mount. His back as straight as a broomstick, he reined around and trotted off.

"Just like him," Evie said with contempt, "to run way instead of face a problem. *Any* problem."

"Forget about him," Emery said. "You're with me now."

"Only until I get bored or someone better-looking wants a tumble."

Fargo had forgotten how much they bickered. "On your horses." He climbed on the Ovaro and when the others were under way, he followed. They had not gone a hundred yards when Evie slowed and paced him.

"Are you proud of me?"

"I'd be happier if you had done as I asked."

"You wouldn't have been alive much longer."

"There's that," Fargo said, and grinned. "Thank you. But you've taken a gamble. The Comancheros might catch us."

"The important thing was you."

"Why?"

"Excuse me?"

"I'm just another in a long string."

"Can't a gal just like someone without it having to be deeper?"

"I suppose," Fargo said. But it bothered him. It bothered him more that he couldn't say why it bothered him. "I hope it doesn't get you killed," he said sincerely.

"It won't."

They rode until twilight through a sea of waving grass. Always, to the west, rose the brown blot on the blue of sky, a constant reminder of the human sharks in their wake.

All that was left of the sun was a golden arch when they came on Adam, who had stopped to wait for them.

"Can we stop for the night? I'm tuckered out."

"We keep going," Fargo said.

"But I'm tired, I tell you."

"Ride."

The sun set. Fargo checked their back trail for sign of a campfire. But the Comancheros hadn't stopped, either.

Stars blossomed and sparkled like gems. The breeze cooled and brought with it the howl of a lonesome wolf.

Chaku was point rider. Evie and Emery were next. Adam trailed them for a while, pouting, but now he came alongside the Ovaro.

"Mind if we talk?"

"About what?" Fargo liked the man about as much as he liked slugs. The kind that crawled on their bellies, not the leaden variety.

"You must think awful poorly of me after what I've done. But you saw how she is. She'll sleep with anyone."

"You didn't know that when you married her?"

"Of course not." Adam sniffed. "I thought she was as pure as the driven snow. Instead she has a heart as black as sin."

"She likes to cavort," Fargo said.

"That's a good word. I didn't think a scout would know a word like that. Yes, she likes to cavort. Although *loves* to cavort is more like it. I asked her the other night how many she has cavorted with and do you know what she told me?"

"She doesn't know."

"Can you believe it? She has lain with so many she has lost count. I need to know. I asked her, was it ten? Twenty? Fifty? Give me some idea. She looked at me and said she remembers a few but the rest meant no more to her than washing her hair except that it felt better."

"Why are you telling me this?" Every now and then Fargo met people who irritated him. Not so much by what they said or what they did but who they were. Adam Yoder irritated the hell out of him.

"I don't want you to think poorly of me."

"Too late."

"I'm serious."

"So am I."

Adam looked away and when he looked back, his eyes were misting. "May I ask why?"

"You whine like a baby. You have pudding for a backbone. You cry at the drop of a pin and you drop the pin. Do you want me to go on?"

"There's more?"

"You are useless in a fight. You can't shoot. You can hardly ride. Did I mention your crying?"

"Yes. That's enough, thank you. I was hoping you were my friend. I could use one right about now."

"You don't thank a man who has just insulted you."

"You were being honest."

"Hell," Fargo said.

"I admit I have a tender heart. But is that so wrong? Just because I'm a man doesn't mean I don't have feelings."

"Most men don't wear them on their sleeve."

"Very well. I won't inflict myself on you any longer," Adam said, sounding hurt. He clucked to his sorrel and rode on ahead.

"I'd kill for whiskey," Fargo said to himself. Come to think of it, he might soon have to kill anyway.

16

By Fargo's reckoning it was three in the morning. Everyone else was asleep. It was his turn to keep watch and he was seated near the horse string. The horses were acting up, pricking their ears and stamping. They had cause. He'd heard the guttural snarl of a big cat. A cougar was prowling around out there.

There was no moon and a lot of clouds. The night was darker than most.

There was no fire, either. Fargo had insisted on a cold camp. A fire would tell the Comancheros where they were. Adam had mewled that he would like some hot food in his belly, so Fargo told him to ride off about a mile and start his own damn fire. That shut Adam up.

The breeze fanned Fargo's face. He stifled a yawn and rose and walked a circle around the horses. They were starting to quiet down. He figured the cougar must be gone.

There was no sign of a fire anywhere to the west. The Comancheros had made a cold camp, too. Maybe because they were close and didn't want their quarry to know. A disquieting notion. He sat back down.

A hint of movement brought Fargo around with the Henry rising and his thumb about to curl back the hammer.

"It's only me," Evie whispered.

"You almost got yourself shot."

Evie sank cross-legged and smiled. "I couldn't sleep. I tried and I tried but I hardly ever can unless I have it first."

"It?" Fargo said, and then realized. "Oh."

"I've always been like this. From the very first time. I don't know what it is about me. Maybe Adam is right and I'm just evil."

"Hell," Fargo said. "His kind call everything they don't like evil, and they don't like a lot."

"So you don't think liking a poke is wrong?"

"No more wrong than breathing."

Evie chuckled. "Thank you. Usually I am content with myself. But Adam went on and on tonight."

"I'm surprised you married him."

"Looking back, so am I. But he was so sweet. It would have been like saying no to a puppy."

Clouds scuttled overhead and in the distance a coyote yipped.

"I would like to get some sleep," Evie remarked. "I'm bushed from all the riding."

"You only have a couple of hours until daylight."

"I know. Which is why I thought you might help."

"Help how?"

"Weren't you paying attention? I sleep better after a poke. Always have. Another quick one like last night."

"Hell," Fargo said.

"What's the matter? I know you liked it. We could sneak off a little ways and you can do me and then I'll sleep like a baby until the break of day."

"Too risky."

"*Life* is a risk. We don't have to go far. Just so they won't hear us if we make more noise than we should."

Fargo thought of her luscious body and her soft lips and hard nipples, and felt a twitch. "I'm thinking about it."

Evie reached over and placed a hand on his thigh. "How about if I help your thinking along?" She ran her hand higher.

The warmth, the tingling. Fargo felt himself growing hard. "You are a distraction."

"I won't distract you long. I promise?" Evie placed her hand on his manhood. "Oh my."

Fargo leaned forward and their mouths met. Her lips were soft cherries, and he loved cherries.

"Mmmm, that was nice," Evie said huskily. "You are about the best kisser ever. Most men don't know how. They just press their lips to a woman's and think that's all there is to it."

"I just do what comes naturally."

"You do it well. It's a shame we aren't in a hotel somewhere so we could spend a week in bed."

Evie kissed him again and by the end of the kiss she was in his lap and he was fondling her and they both were panting.

"Damn. A girl could get used to you if she wasn't careful."

Fargo gazed at the sleepers. Emery was snoring. Adam was curled into a ball. Chaku was on his back, his war club across his chest.

Evie rose and clasped his hand. "Come on. I need it bad."

"Keep your voice down." Fargo stood. She held on to him and pulled him around the horses and a dozen yards into the prairie.

"This should do." Evie faced him and stood so her breasts brushed his chest.

"Take me. However you like."

Fargo set the Henry down. As he straightened he pressed his mouth to her belly and kissed her through her dress. She giggled and removed his hat and ran her fingers through his hair.

"You're playful, too. I like that in a man."

"Did you bring me out here to talk or the other?" Fargo raised his mouth to the base of her throat. Her skin rippled.

"God," Evie breathed. "I want you in me so much."

"Shouldn't keep a lady waiting," Fargo teased, and hiked her dress until it was bunched around her waist. He covered her crinkly bush and she shivered. "You sure do like it."

"You have no idea."

Yes, Fargo did. In that respect she was a lot like him. He ran his fingers down one thigh and up the other and she shifted and parted her legs. The heat she gave off, she was a fire of her own.

"Don't dally, damn you."

"Now, now." Fargo slid his hand over her slit. She was wet for him, wet and hot. He rubbed her tiny knob and she rose onto her toes and arched her back and her mouth opened wide.

"Oh God, I love it so."

Fargo rubbed some more. He inserted a finger and slowly fed it in. She shook, and sucked in a deep breath, and suddenly she was against him, kissing him and caressing him and exploring him. Fargo gave his own carnal craving full rein and for a while there was nothing but soft skin and softer lips and her wet and his hard.

"Please," Evie panted. "Please put it in me. I can't stand not to any longer."

"As the lady wishes," Fargo said in mock gallantry. He freed his rigid member.

Evie gripped him. "You have a beautiful one, you know."

Fargo laughed.

"I'm serious. You wouldn't know. You don't see as many as I do. I would love to cut yours off and keep it with me."

"That was silly," Fargo said. He ran the tip of his member along her slit.

"Think what you want." Evie closed her eyes and her throat bobbed. "Just put it in me. Please. Please. Please."

"You don't have to beg," Fargo said. He positioned himself and rammed in and up.

Evie's eyes opened wide and she raised her face to the clouds and for a moment Fargo thought she was going to scream. She stifled it by burying her teeth in his shoulder. Her arms clamped tight and she thrust against him in a frenzy of desire. Fargo squeezed a breast, pinched a nipple. Evie, breathing heavily, thrust faster and harder. Her sheath was liquid velvet on his sword. Suddenly her whole body went rigid. For a few seconds she was suspended as if frozen in place. Then she exploded, and hers triggered his.

They were a long time coasting to a stop.

Evie slowly unwrapped her legs. Wearing a contented smile, she sank to the ground. "You sure do make a girl feel good."

Fargo was feeling good himself. He hitched his pants and got himself together and sat beside her. Fatigue nipped at him but he shrugged it off.

"I must be loco to do some of the things I do."

"You mean to make love with a passel of Comancheros somewhere close by?"

"I'm like you," Fargo said. "I want it when I want it."

"I don't think you are quite like me," Evie said languidly. "I'll do it with just about anybody. I suspect you are more picky."

"I have a few standards," Fargo said.

"I only have one. I don't like stink. If a man smells, I won't have anything to do with him." Evie giggled. "Yet another reason I took up with Adam. He always smelled so nice and clean. He takes a bath practically every day."

"A great reason to marry someone."

"Maybe not for you. But stink makes me gag and I'd rather not gag when I have a man inside me. It upsets them terrible."

Fargo patted her thigh. "We make it out of this, I might take you up on that hotel."

"Might? I haven't won you over yet?"

Fargo leaned back. He was truly and fully relaxed for the first time in days. But it didn't last. He thought of the Comancheros and felt the tension creep into his gut. "They'll catch us, you know."

"Not if we ride real hard."

"You should have gone on," Fargo said. "You shouldn't have come back for me."

"What kind of person would I be if I ran out on a friend?"

"Is that what we are?"

"I'd like to think so. To you it's probably not much. But for all the poking I let men do, not many are my friends. Most just want to poke and go." Evie's voice softened and she placed her hand on his. "You are my friend, aren't you?"

Fargo sensed it was important to her. "I am if you want me to be."

"Good." Evie closed her eyes and wriggled. "I smell the roses with the best of them."

"You do what?"

"My ma always used to say how we should take time to smell the roses. She was a worker, my ma. She worked from sunup until eight or nine every day of the year. Washing, scrubbing, cooking, mending. But she always took time out. An hour here, an hour there. Smelling the roses, she called it. Well, to me, a poke is a rose."

"I like how you look at things."

"Thank you, sir."

"Sir?"

"Any man who pokes me is entitled to some respect. For a while, anyway." Evie closed her eyes and sighed.

"No falling asleep," Fargo cautioned.

"What? You're worried the Comancheros might sneak up on us?" Evie said dreamily. "You're wide awake and I trust you."

"Some of them have Indian blood."

Evie opened her eyes. "Oh, all right. Help me up. But I do so love a nap, after."

They walked back, her head on his arm. Adam and Emery and Chaku were still asleep, or appeared to be. The horses were undisturbed.

"See? You were worried over nothing." Evie pecked him

on the cheek and said more quietly, "Thank you. I needed that."

"Anytime."

Evie winked and eased onto her blanket. "I'll hold you to that, handsome. Just see if I don't."

The Ovaro whinnied.

Fargo turned and spied several dark shapes low to the ground. In the dark they were vague blobs that might be bushes, except that he knew no bushes had been there when he went off with Evie. He stabbed his hand for his Colt and went to shout but a hand was clamped over his mouth from behind even as a strong arm was wrapped around his middle.

Fargo drove his head back and connected with a nose. He hooked his elbow into ribs and brought his boot down on an instep. The man holding him staggered.

Again he clawed for his Colt, bellowing, "Comancheros!" to warn Chaku and the stepbrothers. Too late, he saw that they were being swarmed. Emery and Adam and even Evie were pinned, but Chaku had gained his knees and was heaving foes with one hand and bashing them with his club with the other.

The night disgorged more of them.

Fargo was mad at himself. His dalliance with Evie was to blame. If he had stayed put and stayed alert, he could have forewarned them. He punched. He kicked. A pair of beefy Comancheros imitated an avalanche. They swept him off his feet and slammed him to the ground with them on top. He connected with a boot to a gut and gave the other a taste of knuckles. Hands from nowhere grabbed his wrists.

Fargo struggled in vain. Comancheros had hold of his arms, his legs.

Chaku was still fighting. His war club was wreaking havoc. He smashed a head, crushed a shoulder. He spun toward another man and raised his weapon to strike.

It was Wilson. His hands flashed and his revolvers cleared

leather and boomed. Shot in midswing, Chaku sprawled to the earth and didn't move.

"So much for the darkie," Wilson said, and twirled his six-shooters into their holsters.

Emery was cursing. Evie had slumped in despair.

A figure in a sombrero reared over Fargo.

"We meet again, amigo," Santos said.

Fargo glared.

"I must hand it to you, as you gringos say. You gave us a run. But now it is over. All that is left is for you to die."

17

Trussed hand and foot, Fargo lay on his side near one of three fires the Comancheros had going. They were celebrating. A bottle was being passed around. They were joking and laughing.

Emery was also tied. He kept straining and swearing.

Adam was on all fours. The leash was around his neck. Santos was amusing himself by feeding Adam bits of antelope meat.

"Look at him," Emery growled in disgust. "I'd die before I'd let anyone do that to me."

Evie, likewise bound, curled her legs under her and sat up. "How do I look?" she asked.

"What the hell kind of question is that to ask at a time like this?"

"Do you think he'll want me?"

"Who?" Emery said, then swore some more. "You whore. You're no better than my worthless stepbrother."

"I like breathing."

Emery twisted toward Fargo. "Will you listen to her? To think I almost made the same mistake Adam did."

"We all make mistakes." Fargo was thinking of how Chaku might still be alive if he hadn't gone off with Evie.

"It's not a mistake to do whatever it takes to live," Evie said.

Emery glowered. "You're a horse's ass. Thank God I finally realize the truth."

"Be nice. I make the best of what life throws at me, is all. You can't blame a person for that."

"If I had a rock I'd beat you with it."

"Now, see. That's why you and me would never work out. You carp too much. You have to learn to enjoy life more."

"You stupid bitch. I'm about to be killed. What the hell is there to enjoy in that?"

"Enjoy each breath until you breathe your last." Evie smiled. "I do declare. I think I just summed up my life."

"God," Emery said.

"You're too bitter inside. It's made you sour."

Emery turned to Fargo again. "Say something. Tell her how stupid she's being."

"Kettle and pot," Fargo said.

"What? You think I have no right to talk? Fine. Stand up for her. You're as stupid as she is."

Wilson strolled over, his sneer as vicious as the rest of him. "All the trouble you went to, and where did it get you?" He laughed.

"You damned white filth," Emery said. "Cut me loose and I'll pound your teeth down your throat."

Wilson stooped and his right hand flicked and he hit Emery across the head with the barrel of his revolver. Emery went limp. "I can't wait to cut this one up," he said, twirling the six-gun into its holster.

Evie sat so her bosom was trying to climb out of her dress. "What about me? Do you want to cut me up, too?"

"You ran off with them."

"They made me."

"You expect me to believe that?"

"How many times have I told you that you're the only man for me? That you excite me like no other?" Evie gave her head a toss and her hair shimmered in the firelight. "Please. Can't we go back to being as we were?"

"It's not for me to say."

"Ask Santos. Tell him my father-in-law hired the scout to come find me. It wasn't my doing."

Wilson reached down and cupped her chin and looked into her eyes. "I might just do that. It would be a shame to lose the best piece I've ever had."

Evie smiled seductively. "I'll make it up to you. I'll do you as I've never done anyone. We'll be in bed for a week."

"You are the most shameless slut I've ever met. I like that about you."

"Save me, Elisha, please."

Wilson swore and cuffed her across the face. "What did I tell you about using my first name where others can hear?"

"Sorry," Evie said contritely, hanging her head. "It's just that I care for you so much."

The gun shark straightened. "I'll see what I can do. But don't get your hopes up. Santos is out for blood." He walked off, his spurs jingling.

"God, I hate myself," Evie said.

"You grovel well," Fargo remarked.

"Please don't think ill of me. If they untie me, I might be able to help you. I can't do anything like this."

"Don't pretend you're doing it for me."

Evie stared at him. "Most men go around with blinders on. I didn't take you for one of them."

After that, nothing was said until another figure rose and sauntered over. Or, rather, two figures; one was on a leash.

Santos wore his oily smile proudly. "Sit, Dog," he commanded, and when Adam obeyed, Santos patted his head. "When we get back I am going to teach him to lick himself."

"Then you're letting him live?" Evie said.

"*Sí.* He is so much a coward, he amuses me." Santos lost his smile. "You, however, senorita, do not. Wilson has asked me to spare you. Give me a reason why I should."

"You're sparing Adam."

"Only until he stops amusing me." Santos rubbed Adam under his chin. "Who can say when that will be?"

"Then spare me to be generous."

"Senorita, of the many traits I have, generous is not one of them. To be generous is to be weak, and my pack of wolves will not follow a weakling. They would rip me to pieces."

"Then do it because Wilson asked you and he's your friend."

"He is no such thing. He is a fellow wolf. All of them are. None are what you would call a friend."

"God, you must be a lonely man."

"I have my Dog," Santos said, and petted Adam.

Fargo raised his head. "How about me?"

"You, gringo, are in for the worst death a man can suffer. I have thought about staking you out and skinning you but I have done that to others many times. I would like to try a new way."

"Will it be here or at your canyon?"

"Are you in a hurry to die?" Santos chuckled. "I will take you back so everyone can see. We will eat and drink and make merry, as you gringos say, and then kill you." He turned and tugged on the leash. "Heel, Dog."

"I'm sorry," Evie said to Fargo. "But the good news is that you won't die tonight."

It was good news. Fargo would have several days to try and get away. But given that the Comancheros would keep him tied and under guard, it would take some doing. He had been trying to loosen the rope around his boots so he could get at the toothpick but the knots were too tight. He decided to wait until most of his captors were asleep.

The celebration went on for another hour. At one point Santos had Adam beg for food and roll over. He had Adam lick his boots clean. The Comancheros howled.

Emery had come around by then. "If it's the last thing I do on this earth, I'm going to kill him. So help me God."

"You'd kill a member of your own family?" Evie said in horror.

"He's not kin by blood. He's nothing to me except an embarrassment," Emery spat.

"That's hardly a reason."

"What do you know, you dumb cow? All you care about is sex. Sex with anyone."

"You didn't mind that once."

"Once," Emery said bitterly. "I thought a woman only did it because she was in love. It never occurred to me a woman would do it just to do it."

"That's why a lot of men do it."

"You're not a man."

"What's good for the gander isn't good for the goose? Men can be with any woman they want but women have to stick to one man?"

"If the woman is decent she does."

"What does that make men?"

Emery started to say something but stopped. He scowled and said harshly, "Don't talk to me, whore."

"How about you?" Evie said to Fargo. "Do you think a woman should only ever be with one man and one man only?"

"Depends on the woman." Fargo grinned. "But I'm glad many don't. Sheep don't appeal to me."

Evie blinked, then laughed. "God, I like you. You make me laugh a lot. You're not just a clod in buckskins."

Fargo thought of Chaku again. "I'm clod enough."

The camp was calming down. Some of the Comancheros turned in. Others sat up talking. Several played cards. Two of the fires were allowed to burn low. Snores rumbled in nocturnal chorus.

Wilson came over to Evie. "I'm about to catch some shuteye. Wanted you to know that Santos says he'll decide what to do with you by morning. He wants to think on it some."

"Thank you for trying."

"I didn't do it for you. I did it for me. You are better in bed than any gal I've ever had."

"A fine compliment."

"You're also damn weird." Wilson wheeled away.

In a while only two Comancheros were still up. They took turns sitting at the fire and sipping coffee or walking the perimeter. Neither paid much attention to their captives.

Fargo let half an hour go by to ensure that everyone who had crawled under a blanket was asleep and then he commenced to twist his arms and pry and tug. He twisted so furiously he chafed his skin raw. Drops of blood trickled down his hand. Which was exactly what he wanted. Blood made the rope slippery and slippery ropes were easier to work out of.

Evie had lain down a while ago and her chest was gently rising and falling.

Emery hadn't moved since his last insult.

Fargo went on rubbing and twisting. The bleeding was worse but he didn't stop. A little blood was nothing compared to dying.

Both sentries were at the fire. Suddenly one stood and came toward them. Fargo froze, his eyelids cracked. All the man did was look at them and continue on his round of the camp.

Fargo resumed working his wrists.

A shooting star cleaved the heavens. A kit fox raised its cry.

Fargo's wrists were in excruciating pain. More scars for his collection, he thought. That was when he noticed Emery was watching him. "Took you to be asleep," he whispered.

"I've been biding my time. They're not as smart as they think they are. I tricked them."

"How?"

"When they tied me I bent my wrists so there was more slack when they were done."

Fargo had tried the same trick but the Comanchero tying him had noticed and forced him to hold his wrists straight.

"Give me a bit and I'll have my hands free," Emery whispered. "Then I'll kill Evie and we can light a shuck."

"You do that, we'll never get away."

"I'll do it quiet," Emery whispered. "Strangle her with my belt. It will be over before you know it."

"I won't let you," Fargo said.

"You can't stop me." Emery's shoulders moved and he pumped his elbows. "Almost there."

Fargo didn't doubt for a second that Emery would do as he said. He wrenched on the rope.

"I only wish I could take my time," Emery was saying. "She deserves to die slow, in a lot of pain."

It occurred to Fargo that Emery sounded just like Santos. "All I have to do to stop you is yell."

"You do that, they'll retie me so I can't escape and I won't be able to free you."

"I won't let you hurt her," Fargo stressed.

"Aren't you sweet?"

"Yes, he is," Evie said, and sat up. "I heard everything, you rotten son of a bitch."

"So what?" Emery said.

"So Skye doesn't have to give a yell. I will. And when I tell the Comancheros, they'll settle your hash, permanent."

"God, I hate you."

Fargo was so intent on them that he nearly jumped when fingers touched his arm and a voice said in his ear, "I will free you." He glanced over his shoulder in shock.

It was Chaku.

18

Chaku had his knife. He cut at the rope around Fargo's wrists. He cut slowly, with great deliberation, as if it took all his will to accomplish.

"Almost there," Emery said again.

"I'm warning you," Evie said.

Fargo exerted all his strength. The rope was parting. Every slice of Chaku's knife severed more strands.

"I want your word you won't try to hurt me or I will shout my head off. I mean it."

"Go to hell, bitch."

"After you," Evie responded. She tilted her head back and opened her mouth.

"All right," Emery said.

Evie lowered her head partway. "I don't believe you. You agreed too easy."

"Damn it, woman. You have my word. Have you ever known me to break it?"

"I've known you to lie. You lied to Fargo about why you wanted to come after Adam and me."

"That's wasn't a lie," Emery said. "I didn't tell him the whole truth. There's a difference."

"Not that I can see."

Their bickering worked to Fargo's advantage; the rope gave and his wrists were free. Quickly, he took the knife from Chaku and cut the rope around his ankles, then gave the knife back and drew the Arkansas toothpick from its ankle sheath.

Rising into a crouch, he crept over to Emery, who was glaring at Evie, and pressed the tip of the blade to Emery's throat. "Make another peep and I will cut you ear to ear."

Emery wasn't stupid. He didn't say a thing.

"I'm cutting both of you loose," Fargo whispered. "You're not to move until I say so." He cut Emery's ropes and moved to Evie.

"What about Adam?" she asked.

"What about him?" Fargo glanced at the sentries. They were at the fire. Any moment one would get up and walk the perimeter.

"You have to free him, too."

"Can't," Fargo said. Adam was curled up asleep next to Santos, the leash around his neck, the other end wrapped around Santos's hand.

"You're not suggesting we leave him? It wouldn't be right."

Emery hissed, "What do you care?"

"Shut up," Fargo warned. He slashed her ropes and turned and moved back to where he had been. He was just in time.

One of the sentries stood and crooked a rifle in his elbow. He came toward them, yawning. He started to go by as he had many times before but abruptly stopped.

Fargo tensed. He was ready to leap but he would rather not. The man might yell or utter a death cry. He glanced at the others, trying to figure out what the man saw that had given him pause. Emery and Evie were sitting as they had been all along. Nothing was different. Then he realized the Comanchero was looking at something behind him. He glanced over his shoulder.

Chaku was still there, his head on his arm, not moving.

"Who the hell is that?" the Comanchero said. He lowered his rifle and came closer. "Why, it's that darkie we drug off a ways earlier."

Fargo had to do it, the risk be damned. He lunged and thrust even as he clamped his other hand over the man's mouth and nose. The toothpick went in to the hilt at the base of the throat. Instinctively, the Comanchero tried to pull away and raise his rifle but Fargo held tight, swept a foot behind his legs and bore him to the ground. It happened so swiftly that the man was dead and convulsing before he could think to shoot.

The rest still slept. The other sentry was pouring coffee.

Only when the man stopped moving did Fargo go to Chaku. He had to shake the warrior's shoulder several times before Chaku raised his head.

"How bad are you?"

"I very weak."

"Stay put. I'll be back for you."

"Leave me. I not much use."

Fargo crawled toward the sentry. The man had his back to him and was sipping from a tin cup. Whenever any of the Comancheros rolled over or mumbled in their sleep, Fargo froze. He was almost to the fire when he saw his Henry and Colt lying next to his saddlebags.

The sentry set down the cup and stretched. He gazed toward the horse string and began to turn in a slow circle.

He was looking for the other sentry.

Fargo coiled. In a few moments the man would realize something was wrong.

The Comanchero started to rise.

In a silent bound Fargo was on him. Again he clamped his hand over the mouth and nose. He also wrenched hard on the man's head and stabbed deep into the side of his neck. A fine mist sprayed over the flames, making them hiss.

Fargo held firm as the man sought to break free. The struggle was brief. Fargo quietly lowered the body and looked around.

The sleepers went on sleeping.

Fargo's sleeve and hand were soaked. He wiped his hand and the toothpick on the man's shirt and slid the toothpick into his ankle sheath. He slid the Colt into his holster, grabbed the Henry and his saddlebags and stalked over to the string.

The Ovaro and their other horses were at the near end.

Thank God the Comancheros were lazy bastards, Fargo reflected. They had left the saddles on. He went from animal to animal, untying them, and cat-footed back.

Emery went to rise but Fargo whispered, "Not yet." He bent over Chaku. "Time to go."

"I tell you leave me."

"No."

"I am weak. I be burden."

"I don't desert a pard." Fargo slid an arm under him and lifted. It was like lifting an ox; Chaku was heavy as hell. Fargo got him to his knees and then to his feet. Evie came up on the other side and added her arm to his.

Emery didn't offer to help.

They crept toward the horses, Fargo's nerves tingling. All it would take was for one of the Comancheros to wake up and they wouldn't make it out alive.

Emery tried to pass them and again Fargo whispered, "No."

"Damn you, anyhow."

Chaku uttered a low groan.

Fargo stopped in dread but none of the Comancheros stirred. Nodding at Evie, he walked on. When they came to the horses, he boosted Chaku up. Both Evie and Emery had to help.

Then they were all on their mounts and Fargo reined around, and swore under his breath.

Adam had sat up and was beckoning.

Evie whispered, "He wants us to take him."

For Fargo that would mean climbing down and working his way through the sleeping Comancheros and trying to slip Adam out of the leash without waking Santos.

"Forget the son of a bitch," Emery said.

Fargo dismounted. He moved faster than was wise, but any

of the Comancheros could wake at any moment. He stepped around several and over several and was close enough to Adam that he could see tears of appeal in his eyes. The man would cry over anything.

Santos was on his side, his back to them.

Adam had the presence of mind to take the leash in both hands and hold it slack.

Fargo drew the toothpick. The leash was rawhide and took effort to cut.

Adam held it steady and didn't let it jerk. When it fell away, Adam grabbed Fargo's hand and silently mouthed several words Fargo couldn't make out.

Fargo nodded at the horses. Adam nodded and stood but tripped over his own feet. Fortunately, Fargo was right there and caught hold and steadied him.

Santos rolled onto his back.

For a second Fargo thought the Comanchero leader was awake but Santos's eyes stayed shut. Holding on to Adam, Fargo headed for the horses.

"Thank you," Adam whispered.

"Shut the hell up, you simpleton."

Emery was impatient to be off. He glowered at his step-brother and as Adam went to climb on, said, "If it was up to me, I'd have left you."

Adam looked at Fargo and then at Emery and whispered, "Shut the hell up, you simpleton."

Fargo was about to climb back on the Ovaro when he noticed that Chaku was slumped over and barely hanging on. "Let me help you." He pushed Chaku up. "Do you think you can ride?"

"No."

Fargo didn't think so, either. He took the bay's reins and the Ovaro's reins and walked into the darkness. The others followed. When he had gone far enough, he turned to his saddle and got his rope.

"I have to tie you on. It's the only way. I'm sorry."

"I understand," the warrior said weakly.

"Once we're safe, I'll see about your wounds. I'm no doctor, but if the slugs are still in you, I might be able to dig them out."

"One is still in," Chaku said. "The other went through." He coughed and drops flecked his lips.

"Just so you know," Fargo said. "Wilson is dead. Santos, too. They don't know it yet but they are."

"For me you do this?"

"For both of us."

"You are good friend, white man."

Fargo put a hand on Chaku's shoulder. "Don't die on me, black man. Keep on breathing to spite them."

"I try."

Fargo rode with the bay always at his side. He was worried, but there was nothing else he could do. For a while he rode at a walk and then spurred to a trot. The jostling wasn't good for Chaku, but again, Fargo didn't have a choice. They must put as much distance as they could between them and the Comancheros.

Not two hours of night were left when Fargo drew rein on a bench atop a rocky ridge. Climbing down, he undid the rope and carefully lowered Chaku onto his back. "How are you holding up?" When there was no answer, Fargo felt for a pulse. It was there but oh so weak.

"Is he dead" Evie asked.

"I hope so," Emery said. "I don't like how he cottoned to Fargo, here, when I'm his master."

Fargo felt an icy chill clear down to his marrow. "You don't like that," he said.

"No, I sure as hell don't."

Fargo reached up and pulled him off his horse and hit him. The punch knocked Emery flat. Emery swore and tried to get back up but he only made it to one knee when Fargo clipped him with an uppercut. Fargo would have hit him again but a hand gripped his lower leg.

"He not worth it, friend," Chaku said.

Fargo squatted. "Lie still and rest. I'm going to make a fire so I can take a look at those bullet holes."

"Not smart. Enemies see fire."

"Maybe they will and maybe they won't. But I owe you. You saved our hash back there."

Fargo scoured for fuel. Scattered scrub brush and patches of brown grass had to suffice.

Adam came over, sniffling.

"What the hell are you crying about now?"

"How happy I am to be alive and free of that awful Santos. You wouldn't believe some of the things he did to me."

"I'd believe them but I don't want to hear them. And stop your damn blubbering."

"Why are you mad at me? I haven't done anything."

"You cry real good."

Fargo turned to Chaku. Both holes were above the left nipple about a hand's width apart. Wilson had gone for the heart and in his haste shot high. Fargo raised Chaku and confirmed there was a single exit wound the size of an apple.

"Do we dig it out?" Evie asked.

"We?" Fargo said, thinking maybe she had experience as a nurse. "Have you done this before?"

"By *we* I meant *you*."

"Hell."

"If it upsets you so much, don't dig it out. Wait until we reach a settlement."

"Can't," Fargo said. "Lead poisoning could set in."

"Is it true that's nearly always fatal?"

"You heard right." Fargo had witnessed several instances and seen the intense suffering it caused. He would rather put a bullet in his brain than go through that.

"Fargo," Emery said.

"Not now."

"It's important."

"I said not now, damn it."

"You don't care if the Comancheros catch up?"

Fargo swore and went over. Even though it was dark there was no mistaking the dust cloud half a mile off.

19

As much as Fargo didn't want to, he lifted Chaku onto the bay, tied him so he wouldn't fall off and resumed their flight. Chaku was in bad shape. A hard ride could kill him. It added to the list of things Fargo's had to worry about.

"Damned if we do and damned if we don't."

"What was that?" Evie asked.

"Nothing."

They rode hard. The others understood what was at stake and didn't flag.

Even Adam, although he flounced around on his saddle as if he were five years old and learning to ride for the first time.

When they had put a mile behind them, they stopped and stared back the way they had come.

The starlight bathed a dusky cloud far off.

"They're still after us," Evie said.

"Did you think they wouldn't be?" Adam said.

"I wish I had a gun," Emery remarked, and held out a hand to Fargo. "Let me have one of yours."

"Not a chance in hell."

"Just one. Either the six-shooter or the long gun. Two of us able to fight is better than one."

"Chuck rocks."

"Against rifles and pistols?"

"Maybe they will give up after a while," Evie said.

"Santos won't stop chasing us this side of the grave," Fargo replied. Which didn't leave him with a lot of options.

Adam had been quiet but now he said, "How about if we go on ahead while you stay and delay them like you did before?"

"That worked real well," Fargo said.

"For once I agree with my stepbrother," Emery said. "We'll take the black and be real careful with him."

"Until you're out of my sight. Then you'll dump him and take his horse," Fargo muttered to himself.

"What should we do, then?" Evie asked. "You must have a plan."

"Stay alive," Fargo said. As plans went, it wasn't much but it was better than breathing dirt.

"*That's* your plan? Can't you be more specific?"

"We need to make a stand."

Adam cleared his throat. "Can I go on by myself? I'm not much use in a fight."

"Or at anything else," Emery said.

"Please," Evie pleaded.

Fargo gigged the Ovaro. They were far enough ahead that he could take the time to find the right spot. And once the Comancheros caught up, it would be do or die.

Unfortunately, they soon put the bluff country behind them and were crossing prairie as flat as a flapjack. The only cover was grass, and the short variety, at that. If the Comancheros caught them in the open . . . Fargo didn't like to think of the outcome. He wanted to pick up the pace but their horses were tuckered out.

Evie joined him. "How is poor Chaku?"

"Not well," Fargo answered.

"He'll die if we don't stop, won't he?" Evie fretted.

"Could be," Fargo said. If he was being honest with her, he would say it was a near certainty.

"I don't want his death on my head. What if Adam and I were to wait for the Comancheros? Santos might be content with us and let the rest of you go."

Adam was right behind them and said, "I heard that. I'll be damned if I let them get their hands on me again."

"Don't you care about Chaku?"

"Not a bit," Adam said bluntly. "What is he to me? I hardly know the man. And him a black."

"You sound like Emery," Evie chided.

To nip yet more of their petty squabbling in the bud, Fargo said, "It wouldn't work anyway. Santos won't give up now. He can't."

"Why not?"

"We made a fool of him. He has to catch us to show his men he's fit to lead them."

"Surely he won't chase us all the way to Dallas," Evie scoffed.

"To the ends of the earth," Fargo said. Not that they would get five more miles. He rose in the stirrups. There was nothing to see but flat and more flat.

"I bet you never counted on anything like this when you agreed to come find us," Evie said.

"You'd win that bet."

"In my defense, sometimes we don't realize a mistake is a mistake until after we've made it."

Chaku raised his head and looked dully about him and said something in what Fargo took to be the Katonza tongue.

"Do you need for us to stop?"

"You," Chaku said. "Now I remember. I not in Africa. I am in strange white land."

"Is there anything I can get you? A sip of water from my canteen? Pemmican?"

"He has killed me."

"Who? Wilson? You're not dead yet. As soon as I can, I'll dig out that slug and bandage you. A month from now you'll be your old self."

"No," Chaku said. He raised his head and gave voice to a singsong chant, a sorrowful song that seemed to contain all the sadness in the world. Then he smiled at Fargo and said, "You good friend." His big body sagged and he let out a long sigh.

"Damn." Fargo drew rein and reached over and felt for a pulse again. This time there wasn't any.

"How is he?" Evie asked.

Fargo let out a sigh of his own.

"Oh," Evie said.

They couldn't take the time to bury him. All Fargo could do was lower him and place him on his back with his hands folded across his broad chest.

"Too bad we don't have a parson to say a few words," Evie said.

"What good would that do?" Emery said. "He wasn't no Christian. He was a heathen, for God's sake."

"It would be nice to say something," Evie insisted.

"Ashes to ashes, dust to dust," Adam said.

They rode on at a gallop and didn't stop until their horses were lathered with sweat. Fargo looked back. They had gained a little but nowhere near enough.

"Oh God," Adam mewled. "They're going to catch us, aren't they?"

"Never any doubt," Fargo said.

"Say," Evie said, and pointed to the east. "What's that yonder?"

An orange dot flickered in the ocean of ink.

"A campfire," Fargo said. Either it was far off or it was a small fire. His instincts told him the latter.

"Maybe they're white men," Adam said. "Maybe they can help us."

Fargo remembered coming across the sign of a war party days ago. "Maybe they're Indians and they can still help us."

"Why would redskins lend us a hand?" Emery scoffed. "Hell, you don't even know if they're friendly or hostiles."

"If I'm right, they're Comanches."

Emery laughed. "And you expect them to help us against the Comancheros? Against the men who trade them guns and whatnot?"

"I do," Fargo said, and rode toward the spot of orange.

Evie was the first to overtake him, then Emery and Adam. Instead of following behind, they rode on either side. It was Adam who couldn't contain his curiosity.

"Care to explain what you have in mind? Our lives are at stake, too, after all."

"Not yet," Fargo said.

"Why the hell not?" Emery demanded. "We have Comancheros after us and Comanches in front of us. Either tell us your plan or I'm going my own way."

"Adios."

Emery didn't ride off. He swore and muttered but stayed. "You're going to get us all killed, you bastard."

"Skye knows what he's doing," Evie said.

"*Skye*," Emery mimicked mincingly. "How sweet you have so much confidence in him. I don't."

"This idea you have," Adam brought up, "how would you rate the chances of it working?"

"Flip a coin," Fargo replied.

"That's not very encouraging."

"All I've gone through for you," Emery said to Evie, "and now I'll likely die thanks to the jackass we hired to find you."

"I didn't ask you to come find me. I told you when I left with Adam that it was over between us. You were the one who wouldn't accept that. You were the one who mistook a couple of pokes for true love."

"It was more like six or seven. And most ladies don't spread their legs unless it means something to them."

"I am not most ladies."

"You're not a lady, period."

Fargo had had enough. "Are your ears working?" he said without looking at either of them.

146

"What?" Evie responded.

"Of course they are," Emery snapped.

"Good. Because the next one who opens their mouth, the very next one, male or female, I will pistol-whip."

"Does that include me?" Adam asked.

"It does."

"How can you be so mean?" Evie said.

Fargo drew rein and palmed the Colt. "The very goddamn next one."

Adam went to speak but thought better of it. Evie appeared confused. Emery did as Emery nearly always did; he glared.

"Will wonders never cease?" Fargo said. He twirled the Colt into his holster and slapped his legs against the Ovaro. For the next half an hour he savored rare and blessed silence. It was almost a shame when he had to rein up and announce, "This is as close as we can go."

The fire was several hundred yards away. A figure was huddled by it and sleeping forms were bathed in its glow.

"Can we talk now?" Evie whispered.

"Does the sun rise every morning?"

"Is that yes or no?" Evie asked, and then said, "What do you want us to do? I can help if I have some idea of what you are up to."

Fargo swung down. "I want the three of you to stay put and not make a peep. If those are Comanches yonder and they catch wind of you, you'll wish the Comancheros had caught you."

"Where are you going?" Adam whispered.

"To have a look-see."

"You are crazy as hell," Emery said.

"You hired me." Fargo removed his spurs and put them in his saddlebags.

Levering a round into the Henry, he stalked toward the camp. If the Indians were from a friendly tribe he would have to warn them about the Comancheros. He hoped they weren't.

He hoped they were the most feared and merciless slayers in all the Southwest, save only the Apaches.

When he was near enough that his silhouette might show against the stars, he flattened and crawled.

The warrior at the fire stood and slowly stretched. His features, the paint on his face, how he wore his hair, his buckskins and moccasins—he was a Comanche.

Fargo smiled. He slid backward until it was safe to stand and hurried to the others. "We're in luck," he informed them. "It's a war party, all right."

"You call that luck?" Emery said.

"Oh God," Adam gasped. "They'll torture us and scalp us."

Evie was gnawing on her lower lip. "What now?"

"We wait." Fargo turned to the west. The dust cloud was there but small yet. It would be a while. He hoped not *too* long. It had to be dark for his plan to work. Sunrise would spoil everything.

Adam was fidgeting as if ants were crawling up his britches. "I can't take this. I really can't. I'll go on alone, if you don't mind."

"I do," Fargo told him. The Comanches might hear him ride off.

"You can't shoot me this close to those Indians," Adam gloated, and turned to his animal.

Fargo took a bound and rammed the Henry's muzzle into Adam's gut. Adam gasped and doubled over. Before he could cry out, Fargo struck him over the head with the stock. Adam dropped like a rock. Taking hold of him, Fargo slung him over his horse, belly down. The horse, thank heaven, stood calm during it all.

"Was that necessary?" Evie criticized.

"I liked it," Emery said. "Hit him again. Knock out his teeth and I'll pay you fifty dollars."

"Must you?" Evie objected.

The dust cloud was bigger.

Over at the fire, the Comanche had squatted and was poking at it with a stick.

"All I can say," Evie whispered to Fargo, "is that I hope to hell you know what you're doing."

"You and me both," Fargo said.

20

Fargo was counting on Santos's conceit. The Comancheros were bound to have spotted the fire. Since the fire was small, they would suspect Indians. And since mainly Comanches roamed this region, they had little reason to be afraid. They were on friendly terms with the terrors of the territory.

To the east the sky had brightened a bit but not enough to ruin Fargo's brainstorm.

"They're getting awful close," Evie remarked, her gaze on the dust cloud.

"It's time," Fargo said. "Take Adam and walk your horses north and keep walking until you hear shots."

"What will you be doing?" Evie asked.

"Turning the tables."

"Be careful. Please. For me."

"I'll be careful enough for the two of us."

Evie kissed him full on the mouth, a heavy, wet kiss full of promise. "Stay alive. There's more of those for you if you do." She grinned and winked.

Emery said, "You must think you're the cat's meow."

"Get going." Fargo waited until they were swallowed by the night and then stepped into the Ovaro's stirrups. The Comanche at the fire hadn't noticed the dust cloud yet. He would soon.

Wedging the Henry to his shoulder, Fargo aimed near a sleeping form, held his breath to steady his rifle and smoothly stroked the trigger. The shot kicked up dirt.

The warrior at the fire leaped to his feet and shouted a warning. Other Comanches scrambled erect with their bows and lances in hand and glanced around in confusion.

Fargo fired a second time, into the fire. Sparks flew. A Comanche was stung in the face and howled. Cupping his hand to his mouth, Fargo hollered, "Come and get me, you red sons of bitches!" He howled and yipped, shoved the Henry into the saddle scabbard and galloped like a madman toward the dust cloud.

They came. Like a swarm of riled hornets, the Comanches flew to their warhorses and gave chase.

Fargo counted twenty, thirty, more. He rode full out, pushing the tired Ovaro. Comanche warhorses weren't turtles. Comanches always picked the best, the fleetest. The trick now was to stay ahead of them and stay alive long enough to reach the Comancheros.

An arrow buzzed out of the sky and barely missed. An incredible shot.

Fargo twisted around and fired the Colt. He didn't aim, didn't try to hit them. There wasn't any need.

Fargo lashed the reins. He was keenly aware that a single misstep could spell his doom. A prairie dog hole, a rut, a gully he noticed too late—all could bring the stallion down.

The Comanches were riding close together, save for a few with swifter mounts. Eager to slay, they had pulled ahead.

To the west, awash in pale starlight, the dust cloud was rising into the sky. The Comanches would see it—and, Fargo hoped, take it to be more white men. To convince them of that, he shouted, "Death to all redskins!" and fired.

They shrieked anew.

Fargo must time the next part of his plan just right. Any mistakes and he was a goner. It might tbe he Comanches who did him in. It might be the Comancheros. Either way, dead was dead.

Fargo thought of Evie, who threw herself at anything in

pants, and of Adam, about as worthless as a man could be. All this was because of them. If he died, there was no one to bury him or carve on his headstone *Here lies Skye Fargo, who died a fool.*

The dust cloud resembled a thunderhead. At its base were stick shapes that acquired the substance of men and horses.

Fargo sucked air into his lungs and let loose a war cry that did the Comanches proud. Extending the Colt, he shot into the thick of the Comancheros.

A man went down.

Fargo fired again, and yet a third time. Twisting around, he shot at the Comanches. Then, hauling on the reins, he bent over the saddle horn and galloped to the north for his very life. This was the crucial moment. He must get out from between the two factions before they crashed together.

The Comancheros cursed and yelled and fired at the spot where Fargo's muzzle flash told them he had been. But instead of hitting him, their leaden hailstorm tore into the front ranks of the Comanches. Incensed, the Comanches loosed a swarm of arrows along with scattered rifle shots from the few warriors who had guns.

Men dropped on both sides.

By then they were close enough to see one another but they were so incensed that they didn't slow or stop or think to ask why they were being attacked. Blood had been spilled and they were rabid for revenge and they didn't give a damn who they had to kill.

Fargo saw it all.

Lead slugs and wooden shafts sizzled through the air. The Comancheros had more guns but there were more Comanches. Like opposing waves they smashed into one another. A horrendous din of war whoops and curses and squealing horses filled the air. It was the madness of the melee, every man for himself.

A Comanchero in a sombrero put two slugs into a Comanche. The next second a Comanche sent an arrow into his chest. Another Comanchero shot a Comanche in the face only to have a Comanche run him through with a lance.

Neither side knew the meaning of mercy. Warriors and Comancheros dropped and died, drenching the prairie with their lifeblood.

Fargo had witnessed battles before, but few so savage, so bloody. He began to reload as he watched.

A Comanchero died screaming with an arrow in his throat. A Comanche had the top of his head blown off.

Out of the whirlwind burst two riders, Santos and Wilson. Wilson was in front. He had a revolver in each hand and he dropped Comanches just as fast as he could shoot. Santos covered their backs.

A burly warrior blocked their path and Wilson put two slugs into him. Santos winged a Comanche coming at them with a lance.

They were heading straight for Fargo. He slid a cartridge into the cylinder, plucked another, slid it in. He finished just as Wilson saw him.

"You!"

They fired simultaneously.

Wilson rocked but didn't go down. He was so intent on Fargo that he didn't hear Santos yell a warning. A Comanche was after them, nocking an arrow to a string. Santos fired but missed and the Comanche loosed his shaft.

Wilson was almost to Fargo. He extended both revolvers for the kill.

The very next instant the arrow caught him in the left shoulder, the force nearly unhorsing him. Twisting at the hips, he snapped a shot at the warrior who had fired the arrow. The warrior's face dissolved.

Wilson turned back.

Fargo was ready. At his shot Wilson reeled. At the next Wilson clutched at the saddle horn. After the third Wilson's saddle was empty.

Fargo looked for Santos, thinking to end it once and for all. The Comanchero leader had reined to the west.

Once again Fargo relied on the Ovaro's exceptional stamina. The sky was steadily brightening and he saw Santos glance over a shoulder at him and scowl.

Santos's horse was flagging and he had only himself to blame. He had pushed his men and their mounts all night, and now, when he needed both the most, he was alone on an exhausted horse that couldn't go much farther without collapsing.

Santos drew rein and turned and raised his revolver.

Much as a Comanche might do, Fargo slid onto the side of the Ovaro. Hanging by his elbow hooked over his saddle horn, and his leg, he fired under the stallion's neck. It took great skill to make such a shot. Only someone who had practiced it could hit what he was aiming at. He hit what he was aiming at.

Santos reared in his stirrups. He flung his arms wide and his head snapped back. Another moment, and his body folded in on itself and he oozed to the ground like so much clay.

Fargo had to be sure. He rode up and dismounted and rolled Santos over. The hole between the eyes was all the confirmation he needed.

To the east the battle was winding down.

Fargo didn't care who won. He climbed on and circled to the north to find Evie, Emery and Adam and head for Dallas to claim the rest of the money he was due.

It puzzled Fargo that he saw no sign of them, even after half a mile. They should have gone only a short way.

To the southeast the Comanches were collecting weapons and finishing off the wounded.

Fargo continued to the north, scouring for sign. Soon he

came across fresh hoofprints. The three had been riding in single file. One of them, for reasons Fargo couldn't yet fathom, had broken away and galloped to the northeast. The other two went after him—or her.

Puzzled, Fargo stuck to their trail and presently spied a prone form in the grass. He swung down before the Ovaro came to a stop.

"Hell."

Adam Yoder lay facedown in a pool of scarlet. Where the back of his head should be was a jagged cavity. Someone had beaten him to death with a blunt object.

Fargo swung onto the saddle and kept going. The tracks told him that one of the riders had galloped away and been pursued by the last. "I'm sorry, fella," he said, and forced the Ovaro to a gallop. He hoped against hope but soon spotted a second body.

Evie was on her back. In the middle of her forehead was an ugly wound caused by a blood-covered rock that lay nearby.

Fargo figured she was dead and went to go around when she did the last thing he expected. She opened her eyes.

"Skye? Is that you?"

Fargo was off the Ovaro and on a knee by her side. Taking her hand, he touched her cheek. "It's me."

"Emery," Evie said.

"I know."

"He killed Adam and he's killed me."

"What set him off?"

Evie licked her lips. Her eyelids fluttered and she appeared on the verge of passing out but she rallied and said, "We went north as you told us. Emery started in on me. About how I wasn't a lady. About how I played him for a fool. Adam asked him to stop but he told Adam that anything Adam had to say was of no account."

Fargo was appalled by how pale she had become. "You don't need to go on."

"Yes. I do." Evie sucked in a deep breath. "They argued. I joined in. The next thing I knew, Emery was saying how it would embarrass him something awful if we were to go back to Dallas with him. He'd be a laughingstock for being so fond of me."

"And?" Fargo prompted when she stopped.

"Sorry. I feel so weak." Evie licked her lips. "Emery caught sight of a rock and climbed down to pick it up. He started toward me and Adam moved his horse between us and told Emery to stop. It was probably the bravest thing Adam ever did, and it got him killed. Emery pulled him off the horse and bashed in the back of his head. It was over before I could do anything. Then Emery turned to me and said it was my turn."

Fargo's face was burning. "So you ran."

"I ran like hell. But my horse played out and he caught me and . . ." Evie stopped. "Oh God. I don't want to die."

"He left you like this."

"He rode off laughing." Evie looked into his eyes. "Thank you for the pokes. They are the last I'll ever have."

"You poke nicely," Fargo said.

Evie managed to smile. "It's loco, isn't it? The world, I mean." Those were her final words. Her eyes grew wide and she stared at the rising sun and was gone.

Fargo took the time to dig a shallow grave. The tracks led him east. Within half an hour he spied Emery. Emery glanced back and saw him, and lashed his reins. Fargo held to a walk. The Ovaro was tired. So was Emery's horse, as Emery found out when he pushed it. Its front legs buckled and it crashed down, rolling as it struck. Emery was thrown clear but he landed in front of his horse—which rolled over him. By the time Fargo got there, the horse was back on its feet and snorting in annoyance while Emery lay on his back with his body bent at an unnatural angle.

Fargo drew his Colt.

"No!" Emery cried, and tried to rise. He couldn't. He got

his hands under him but it made no difference. "Oh God. I can't move my legs."

"Well now," Fargo said.

"I think my back is broken. I can't feel anything from my waist down." Emery held out a hand. "Help me up."

Fargo holstered his Colt.

"Didn't you hear me? Help me, damn you. If you don't, I'll starve to death. Or die of thirst."

"The wolves or the coyotes will be here long before then."

"Oh God," Emery bleated. "If they do they'll eat me alive."

"Tell you what," Fargo said. "I will help you, after all." He climbed down and bent and drew the Arkansas toothpick.

"What good will that do me?"

"You, it won't do any good. But the blood will help the wolves and the coyotes find you." Fargo cut deep into Emery's shoulder and blood spurted.

Emery cried out and tried to draw away.

Fargo cut him again, in the arm. "That should do it."

Emery raged and swore and shook his fist.

Fargo wiped the blade clean on the grass and slid the knife into his boot.

He swung onto the Ovaro and smiled and touched his hat brim. "Adios."

Fear filled Emery's eyes. "Wait! Please! You can't just ride off and leave me."

"Watch me," Skye Fargo said, and used his spurs.

LOOKING FORWARD!
The following is the opening section of the next novel in the exciting *Trailsman* series from Signet:

THE TRAILSMAN #344
SIX-GUN GALLOWS

Southwest Kansas Territory, 1860—where "Bleeding Kansas" earns its name in spades when Skye Fargo cleans out an outlaw hellhole.

The Ovaro suddenly gave his trouble whicker, and Skye Fargo, naked as a newborn, shook water from his eyes as he hustled out of the chuckling creek and onto the grassy bank.

His gun belt hung from the limb of a scrub oak, and he filled his hand with blue steel. He clapped his hat on, not wanting to die totally naked. Then he knocked the rawhide riding thong off the hammer and thumb-cocked his single-action Colt.

"Steady, old warhorse," he soothed the nervous pinto stallion. "Let's have a squint—might be just a stray buffalo spooking you."

Staying behind the stunted tree, Fargo used his left hand

to clear his vision of leaves. His face was tanned hickory-nut brown above the darker brown of his close-cropped beard. Eyes the bottomless blue of a mountain lake peered out from the shadow of his broad black plainsman's hat.

Fargo's first glimpse was the infinite vista of the western Kansas Territory plains, so vast and boundless that many men lost their confidence for feeling so dwarfed in it.

A heartbeat later, however, his blood iced when he saw that trouble was boiling to a head.

About a quarter mile north of his well-hidden position at the creek, a small group of pilgrims—perhaps seven families— were traveling west. Fargo recognized their sturdy wagons as the type made famous in Lancaster County, Pennsylvania. And the men's clergy black suits, the women's crisp white starched bonnets, told him they were Quakers.

Pacifists, out here of all places. Fargo mocked no man for his heartfelt religious convictions and tended to like the hard-working, charitable Quakers. But this was the wrong place to turn the other cheek.

And most definitely the wrong time, he thought, watching a boiling yellow-brown dust cloud approaching from the Cimarron River to the north—a large group of riders, and only iron-shod horses would kick up that much dust. Large groups of riders, anywhere in the Kansas Territory, meant hell would be coming with them. This wasn't called Bleeding Kansas for nothing.

"You damn, thick-skulled fools," Fargo said in frustration as he pulled on his buckskin shirt and trousers, then his triple-soled moccasin boots. "This ain't Fiddler's Green out here."

Fargo knew there had been settlement going on for some time in the eastern half of the territory, but lately he had seen more pilgrims like these pushing way too far west—well beyond the U.S. army's protection line. Just some stubborn and isolated homesteaders trying to prove up government land, without permission, in rain-scarce country better suited for grazing.

The Quakers, having spotted the approaching riders, had reined in their teams of oxen. But since defending themselves was not an option, they took no further action—merely waited patiently for whatever fate befell them.

By now Fargo's stomach had fisted into a knot. The riders were close enough that he recognized their butternut-dyed homespun clothing. Border Ruffians . . . organized gangs of supposed antislavers who clashed with the "pukes," similar gangs from Missouri who used pro-slavery rhetoric as a thin excuse to terrorize settlers.

Fargo had waltzed with both factions before: kill-crazy marauders of no-church conscience.

But usually, he reminded himself, they were found well east of here, where the settlers and towns were. This was a long distance from their usual range—a fact that piqued Fargo's curiosity.

"Something ain't jake here, old campaigner," he told the Ovaro, his voice calming the nervous stallion.

First Fargo heard the warbling cries as the attackers moved in, then the sickening sound of a hammering racket of gunfire. Men frantically pushed their women and children into the wagon beds as bullets dropped some of the oxen in their traces.

At least thirty riders, Fargo estimated, all well heeled and liquored up. And he knew damn well these mange pots could take a human life as casually as shooing off a fly. Many had developed a taste for killing during that slaughterfest known as the Mexican War.

After killing a number of the oxen, they took aim at the

butcher beef and milk cows tied to the tailgates of the wagons. Fargo's face etched itself in stone when they next killed every adult male, then pulled some of the screaming girls from the wagons and gang-raped them—innocent girls who had never experienced violence in their lives.

But Fargo stayed hidden despite the anger roiling his guts. It was one of the ugliest scenes he had ever witnessed, but there wasn't a damn thing he could do about it—not now.

He had learned long ago never to push if a thing wouldn't move. He would gladly risk his life to help any man—and especially a woman or child—if there was even the slimmest chance of success. Revealing himself now, however, would simply make him part of the slaughter. Fargo preferred to survive so he could avenge it.

And he vowed that he would. He had been on his way to the sand-hill country of the northern Nebraska panhandle country, hired by the U.S. army to be a fast-messenger rider between military outposts there. But the army could wait— no man worth the name could turn his back on this.

The grisly nightmare was over in about fifteen minutes. At least the marauders hadn't killed any women or children. When the attackers had cleared out, after only quickly looting the wagons, Fargo untied the Ovaro's rawhide hobbles and vaulted into the saddle.

"Jesus, I could use a drink," he informed the landscape as he cleared the scrub oaks and cantered the Ovaro toward the scene of devastation.

The sights—and especially the god-awful sounds—forced Fargo to all his reserves of strength. The survivors had gathered around dead and dying men, their cries piteous. Girls who had been brutally raped lay in wide-eyed shock, young children bawled like bay steers, frightened out of their wits. Despite his best effort, Fargo misted up.

An elderly woman spotted him riding in and screamed. "Please, God, no more!" she begged the heavens. "Thou must please make him leave us alone!"

Fargo realized she had confused his fawn-colored buckskins with butternut.

"I'm a friend, ma'am," he assured her. "I'm not part of that bunch that just left."

"Friend?" she repeated in a tone implying she no longer trusted the word. Then she turned away and folded to the ground, overcome with grief.

A man lay slumped on the box of his wagon, screaming in agony. Fargo hauled back on the Ovaro's reins and threw a leg over the cantle, dismounting. He threw the reins forward to hold his pinto, then checked on the man. He'd been gutshot twice and was past all help. All that lay in store for him was hours of indescribable agony while he bled out.

His face set hard as a steel trap, Fargo moved out of the man's line of sight, shucked out his Colt, then sent the man to glory with a clean head shot. He expected howls of protest, but this bunch were in such shock no one took notice.

"Listen, folks!" Fargo shouted. "We'll have to bury your dead and get you out of here. Even if that gang of white men are done with you, the Indian Territory is only forty miles south of here, and some of the hotheads like to jump the rez. There's dozens of tribes there, and warpath braves could be anywhere in this area."

No one seemed to be listening. Fargo grabbed a shovel from a wagon and began digging a mass grave. Soon a few women and older boys had joined him. The elderly woman Fargo had first spoken to had recovered from the worst of her shock and spoke a prayer after the bodies had been covered with dirt.

"We thank thee, young man," she said to Fargo. "We came

out from western Pennsylvania. We never expected anything like this. No one warned us. We're just farmers."

Fargo felt a welling of hopelessness. How many times had he heard those fateful words on the lips of green-antlered settlers burying their dead?

"What brought you folks this far out, ma'am?"

"Well, all the talk of railroads. We hoped to prosper."

Railroads. Fargo had all he could do not to curse. There were still no railroads west of the Missouri River, but plenty of misguided folks were riding west on rumor waves. In 1854 the Committee on Territories proposed building three transcontinental lines, two of them slicing through the entire width of Kansas. Squatters immediately began pouring into the area. Some were the usual profiteers who hoped to cash in by being first on the scene. Others, like these folks, were hapless farmers expecting new markets for their crops—and finding only a nameless grave like this one.

But Fargo looked at this tired old woman, her eyes watergalled from weeping, and dropped the matter.

"Ma'am, obviously you folks are in no shape to push on. Fifteen miles east of the Cimarron River, there's a trading post called Sublette. There's clean water, plenty of room to camp and plenty of protection if you join with other settlers. There's also experienced guides for hire if you decide to go home."

The woman nodded. "My name is Esther Emmerick. Who were those men who . . . who attacked us?"

Again that question niggled at Fargo. "Well, they sure looked like Kansas Border Ruffians. But this is mighty far west for them."

"I've heard of them—supposedly they are looters. These men hardly touched our possessions."

"Yeah, I noticed that, too," Fargo said. "It's a mite curious, isn't it?"

The old matriarch steeled her resolve with a mighty sigh. "We're in God's hands for good or ill. Will thou take us to this trading post, Mr. . . ."

"Fargo. You better believe I will. I'm on a mission for the U.S. Army, but it can wait."

"Army? Thou art a solider?"

"No, ma'am. I do contract work for them now and then. Scouting, hunting, messenger, in that line."

"I see. One moment, please, Mr. Fargo."

The woman went to a nearby wagon, rummaged in the back and returned with a doeskin pouch. It was sewn shut with thick gut string.

"Two nights ago," she explained, "a badly wounded soldier, barely able to walk, met up with our group. The poor man died, but before he did he gave this to my—my husband—"

Her eyes cut to the new grave, but then she forged on. "He could barely speak, but he said it was imperative that this pouch be delivered to a military officer—*only* an officer. He said it must not be opened before such delivery. Thou, Mr. Fargo, art more likely to see an officer before I do. May I trust it to thee?"

Fargo took it, noticing dried blood all over it. "It feels empty," he remarked.

"Yes, but that poor soldier was adamant that it be delivered."

"I'll take care of it," Fargo promised.

He glanced around. A westering sun threw long, flat shadows to the east.

"All right, folks, I know it's hard for you, but we have to get a wiggle on. If you rehitch some of the teams, there should be at least one ox for every wagon."

Nobody moved, not wanting to leave the grave. Most stood still as stone lions, staring at the new mound of dirt. Fargo hated to get rough with them, but there was no other way to save them.

"Damn it, people, stir your stumps!" he snapped. "What's done is done. Do you want the children to die, too?"

That finally goaded them into action. Feeling like a brutal mine foreman, Fargo began helping the women with their teams. But he vowed to move heaven and earth, if that was what it took, to punish every murdering son of a bitch who had attacked these helpless innocents.

No other series packs this much heat!

THE TRAILSMAN

#320: OREGON OUTRAGE
#321: FLATHEAD FURY
#322: APACHE AMBUSH
#323: WYOMING DEATHTRAP
#324: CALIFORNIA CRACKDOWN
#325: SEMINOLE SHOWDOWN
#326: SILVER MOUNTAIN SLAUGHTER
#327: IDAHO GOLD FEVER
#328: TEXAS TRIGGERS
#329: BAYOU TRACKDOWN
#330: TUCSON TYRANT
#331: NORTHWOODS NIGHTMARE
#332: BEARTOOTH INCIDENT
#333: BLACK HILLS BADMAN
#334: COLORADO CLASH
#335: RIVERBOAT RAMPAGE
#336: UTAH OUTLAWS
#337: SILVER SHOWDOWN
#338: TEXAS TRACKDOWN
#339: RED RIVER RECKONING
#340: HANNIBAL RISING
#341: SIERRA SIX-GUNS
#342: ROCKY MOUNTAIN REVENGE

**Follow the trail of the gun-slinging heroes of
Penguin's Action Westerns at
penguin.com/actionwesterns**

S310